From Oil to Lithium: Navigating the Future of Energy

A Journey from
BLACK GOLD
to
WHITE GOLD

KULDEEP GUPTA

BLUEROSE PUBLISHERS
India | U.K.

Copyright © Kuldeep Gupta 2024

All rights reserved by author. No part of this publication may be reproduced, stored in a retrieval system or transmitted in any form or by any means, electronic, mechanical, photocopying, recording or otherwise, without the prior permission of the author. Although every precaution has been taken to verify the accuracy of the information contained herein, the publisher assume no responsibility for any errors or omissions. No liability is assumed for damages that may result from the use of information contained within.

BlueRose Publishers takes no responsibility for any damages, losses, or liabilities that may arise from the use or misuse of the information, products, or services provided in this publication.

For permissions requests or inquiries regarding this publication, please contact:

BLUEROSE PUBLISHERS
www.BlueRoseONE.com
info@bluerosepublishers.com
+91 8882 898 898
+4407342408967

ISBN: 978-93-6452-779-8

Cover design: Tahira
Typesetting: Tanya Raj Upadhyay

First Edition: August 2024

Disclaimer

The characters, events, and situations depicted in this book are entirely fictional. A resemblance to actual persons, living or dead, or to actual events or locales is purely coincidental.

The author and publisher do not endorse any actions or behaviors portrayed in this work of fiction. The narrative is intended for entertainment purposes only and should not be interpreted as advice or guidance in real-life situations.

Readers are advised that the content may contain themes, language, or situations that some may find objectionable. The views and opinions expressed within this book are those of the characters and do not necessarily reflect the views of the author or publisher.

Any reliance you place on such information is therefore strictly at your own risk. In no event will author or publisher be liable for any loss or damage including without limitation, indirect or consequential loss or damage.

By reading this book, you acknowledge that you understand its fictional nature and accept all responsibility for your interpretation of its content.

Witnessing the Transition of Century

"One revolutionary Transition happened when Human mobility switched from Bullock cart to Engines and another revolutionary Transition is happening when Human Mobility is switching from Engines to Batteries"

An Era of Black Gold is turning in Era of White Gold

Chapter 01: Beginning of Adventurous Life of Black Gold

Standing before Terminal 3 of Indira Gandhi International Airport, Karan could feel his heart beating fast with excitement and apprehension. The ceilings of the terminal were high, and the space was full of moving passengers, each immersed in their personal missions. But for Karan, the world seemed to be moving in slow motion. This was his moment of calling—something he had been preparing for since his student days at the University of Petroleum and Energy Studies in Dehradun.

The airport buzzed with activity. Families hugged and cried silently, people in business talked in hushed tones during their last calls, and young tourists clutched their tickets like precious jewels. The digital display board blinked before Karan's eyes, showing his flight number, poised to take off like a creature waiting for the moon outside its den. With each flash of light in the pitch-black darkness, he felt a step closer to his future—a future that promised adventure, success, and a fresh start.

As he waited, Karan's thoughts began to trace the path he had taken. It all started in 2006 at the University of Petroleum and Energy Studies in Dehradun, where he pursued a degree in Petroleum Engineering. The serene environment, with deep green landscapes and the Mussoorie mountain ranges visible from almost every corner of the campus, had always left a lasting impression on him.

Karan's upbringing influenced his entry into the field of petroleum engineering. He came from a relatively educated family of engineers and scientists. His father, also an engineer, often discussed how energy was the wheel that kept the economies of the world moving. Growing up, these discussions intrigued Karan and fueled his desire to be part of the energy sector. He would sit attentively, listening and asking questions about how things operated and why energy was so significant.

One vivid memory from Karan's childhood was when he was in the 7th grade and had the opportunity to visit his uncle's place in Panipat. His uncle worked at the Indian Oil Refinery in Panipat and one day took Karan to the refinery plant. Karan was fascinated by the vastness of the refinery, which spread over hectares of land. The large equipment used for different processes of refining crude oil captivated him. His uncle arranged for Karan to have a full tour of the refinery with the supervisors. Karan saw enormous oil tanks, towering columns, and a complex structure of pipelines where several men were working. The supervisors explained that the refinery operated day and night, never stopping unless for maintenance work, and that people worked in shifts. It was a massive facility, and although Karan grew tired from walking, his curiosity only increased.

The supervisor patiently answered Karan's many questions, some of which might have seemed silly, but he appreciated the boy's curiosity and eagerness to learn. After the tour, Later, Karan rejoined his uncle, still full of questions. "Uncle, where do we get all this crude oil from? And how do we sell it?"

His uncle smiled, and said "Well, Karan, the government is the one that buys the crude oil for refineries like this one. Once it's refined, we sell it to petrol pumps through distributors in the city." Karan nodded, absorbing the information. This experience sparked Karan's motivation to pursue a career in the Oil & Gas industry.

Karan, being a diligent student of history, was particularly intrigued by the role crude oil played in shaping the outcomes of World War I and World War II. Oil was the lifeblood of war; those who controlled the flow of "black gold" held a significant advantage. Tanks, submarines, and aircraft were all powered by crude oil, making it a decisive factor in both wars. Each country's war strategy was largely determined by the availability and quality of its oil reserves, and the desperate attempts to secure more. Limiting access to oil meant limiting the war itself, a reality that would go on to reshape not only the future of the oil and gas industries but also the geopolitical landscape of the entire world. Karan learned from the history of the world wars that fighter planes, bombers, tanks, battleships, submarines, and supply trucks were all highly energy-intensive. For example, a tank achieved a fuel economy of around 0.5 miles per gallon. Erwin Rommel once wrote, "Neither guns nor ammunition are of much use in modern warfare unless there is sufficient petrol to haul them around… a shortage of petrol is enough to make one weep."

Karan also learned that the Second World War was a war of motion. Overall, America's forces in Europe used 100 times more gasoline in World War II than in World War I. In 1944, General Patton berated Eisenhower, saying, "My men can eat their belts, but my tanks gotta have gas." Securing oil dictated each country's war strategy, which is why Germany attacked Russia. In fact, all modern wars are also fought for oil and gas. Hitler told Mussolini, "The life of the Axis depends on those oilfields." For everything, energy was needed to make it work, and in the 20th and 21st centuries, energy was synonymous with oil and gas. Karan was deeply interested in energy—energy was everything for people and machines. These stories motivated Karan to pursue a career in Oil & Gas. From an early age, he started reading about crude oil's extraction, transportation, and refining, and how it played a significant role in people's lives. This glimpse into the world of petroleum stirred something deep within him.

That day marked the beginning of Karan's deep interest in energy as a field of study. He immersed himself in books and documentaries about oil and gas, drawn to the endless challenges and the immense scale of the industry. The feeling of belonging to a group of people who provided energy to the entire world enticed him. He dreamed himself drilling for oil, exploring new fields, and ultimately contributing to the global energy supply.

Science and technology were Karan's favorite subjects during high school. He enjoyed physics and chemistry, sometimes staying up late at night conducting experiments and reading about recent developments in energy. His teachers noticed his passion and encouraged him to further his learning in that area.

So, when the time came for him to decide on his field of study for higher education, petroleum engineering was the obvious choice. Even though Karan was interested in the subject, he was also motivated by the real-world facts. He understood that the energy sector had spectacular prospects for development and expansion. It was a field where he could do something useful for people and simultaneously be helpful for himself.

The noise at Terminal 3 reached a new intensity. The atmosphere was a vibrant mix of colors and cultures as people from all walks of life hurried through the terminal. Everywhere Karan looked, he saw a diverse array of ethnicities—Africans, Europeans, and Asians—each absorbed in their own journey.

Karan could feel the beginning of a new life. He and Tushar continuously talked about their future "black gold" careers and how fortunate they were to be in this field. Karan finally checked in for his Air India flight; his ticket was like a jewel. It was an immense pleasure for Karan to see his name on the boarding pass, with a flight from Delhi to Dubai. He immediately took a picture of the ticket on his phone and proceeded to immigration. This was his first immigration experience, and everyone, including Karan, was nervous about what the immigration officer would ask.

Those who crossed the immigration checkpoint felt like they had won a war. When Karan's turn came, the immigration officer asked about his trip to the UAE. Karan proudly replied that he had been recruited and was going to work on an offshore rig. The immigration officer glanced at him and then stamped his passport. Everything started changing in Karan's mind as he became super excited to proceed to the security check-in. After completing the security check, they all sat at the designated gate two hours before the flight. Tushar left to use the washroom and asked Karan for a coffee. Karan agreed, and Tushar went off.

Meanwhile, Rishabh and Shahil were deep in conversation, as both were from Dehradun. Harshit was busy talking to his girlfriend. He was also from a small town in Uttarakhand. Karan's mind began to drift back to his college days, recalling his first year at the University of Petroleum and Energy Studies.

Karan remembered his first day on campus when he started his journey into the life of "black gold." The weather in Dehradun was moderate, though cold most of the time, with a bit of warmth during some parts of the year and occasional summer showers. Karan felt elated every time he looked at the greenery around him; it was beautiful, and the scenery from his hostel was breathtaking. His hostel was in the forest of a village in Bidholi,

15 km away from the Indian Military Academy in Dehradun.

In the first year, Karan joined a race to achieve good grades, secure a job, establish himself, and earn the pride of his family, relatives, and friend.

One of Karan's pivotal decisions was to stay in the hostel, which had a tremendous impact on his college life. During the first year, he tried to learn as much as possible and get close to his professors. He was punctual, enjoying early morning classes, avoiding mass bunking, and attending all classes. The major subjects of the first-year curriculum in petroleum engineering were similar to those of other engineering branches, though geology was an extra course. Geology fascinated Karan; he was keen to read books on rocks and the earth's surface history. He was enthralled by exploring how crude oil is found beneath the earth's surface.

Ragging was a common practice during the first year. After classes, first-year students were often summoned by seniors to crack jokes, perform dances, and mimic others for entertainment. They were also made to write inappropriate one-liners about female lecturers, complete seniors' homework, and endure other humiliating tasks. Initially, Karan felt embarrassed witnessing these rituals, but he took it in stride, knowing that the next year, he would be the one in charge

However, Karan did socialise and found friends who were kind and did not indulge in ragging. His closest friend was Rahul Dsouza, who was with him most of the time. They discussed dreams, fears, and togetherness—the camaraderie that helps during the difficult times of college life. Rahul was in Aerospace Engineering, fun-loving, hard-working, and at the top of his class. Their third flatmate was in the same branch as Karan. The three of them became close friends, enjoying and enduring the experiences of hostel life together.

While education was essential to college, it wasn't the only focus. College life was like a kaleidoscope, with intricate elements drawn from different perspectives, individuals, and emotions. For Karan, the University of Petroleum and Energy Studies offered more than just academic learning—it opened up a new experiential world filled with friendships, social relationships, and multicultural interactions.

Courses such as BBA and MBA were less time-consuming than the intensive engineering programs. These programs were also known for attracting beautiful and charming students, many of whom were locals from Dehradun and its surrounding areas. Their lively presence filled the campus with energy and colour, illuminating university life.

When talking about the climate, everyone knew that Dehradun's weather was volatile; in fact, there was a famous saying that, like Dehradun's weather, even women could change at any moment. This saying generally held some truth, as the girls from the region were usually lively and stunning. Their joyfulness and conversations made the campus vibrant, something Karan found irresistible and harmless.

Still, Karan found himself drawn to this new world. The interactions mattered; the prospect of making new friends and the stunning and mysteriously alluring local girls pulled him in. He loved the informal interactions within the grassy areas of the university, the social interactions in the canteen, and the cultural activities involving students from different courses.

He had a clear vision of his future and understood that the primary reason for his presence at the university was to excel in petroleum engineering. The career path he had set his heart on required hard work and commitment, and he wasn't willing to let anything stand in the way of his plans.

At times, though, he didn't go about his daily routine with such equanimity. He recalled the evenings spent with his peers, strolling through the lawns where students from different courses gathered. The BBA and MBA students would often compare their schedules, which were rigorous during the weekdays, as well as their weekend plans and night outs. Though Karan was interested in these conversations, he never lost sight of the goals he wanted to achieve.

He also couldn't deny that the students from these courses were often more innovative and organised some of the best events on campus. Cultural festivals, talent shows, and sports meets were activities mainly spearheaded by the MBA and BBA students, and the energy they put in was filled with passion. Although Karan attended these events, he appreciated the break they provided from his rigorous study schedule. He admired the orderliness and creativity of the students he met, who often engaged him in informal conversations that included jokes and critical thinking about future occupations.

His interactions with his batchmates from these courses also made him aware of crucial social behaviours. These interactions not only added value to his college years but also gave him a well-rounded outlook that embraced not only the subjects he studied but also aspects he hadn't learned in his classes.

However, there was a silver lining in everything that happened to Karan—his determination to succeed academically never wavered. In his first year of college, he was also a regular at the library, dedicating hours to research and other projects. He knew that his task in his petroleum engineering course was challenging, and he was aware that his future growth depended on the effort he was putting into the course. He wanted to socialise with friends but was more focused on ensuring his academics paid off.

This tension between academic and social commitments was delicate but healthy, and Karan managed it wisely. He also realized the importance of having fun but didn't let it overshadow his objectives. Karan understood that this balance would help him not only in college but also in his future endeavours.

The academic week was hectic, but there was enough time to ease the pressure from Friday evening to Sunday. Some colleges offered bus services that shuttled students to the city in the morning and returned by evening. Karan and his friends often visited Dehradun, an active town frequented by students from different colleges. They would go to the famous Paltan Bazaar, a narrow street in front of the Clock Tower, the centre point of Dehradun for their stationery needs. They shopped in Paltan Bazaar for their daily needs and stationery supplies at small shops run by local small-scale business owners. It would be unfair not to mention the famous Rajpur Road, known for many reasons: it leads to Mussoorie and passes by famous schools like Doon School and Welham Girls' School—institutions known for educating the elite. Many celebrities' children have studied or are studying at these schools. Admission to these schools requires hefty fees and strong financial and social backgrounds. Rajpur Road is a long road with major brand showrooms and malls lining both sides, taking you directly to the Queen of the Hills. Karan and his friends would shop as needed, enjoy local food, stroll down Rajpur Road, and finally board the college bus to return to the hostel. Near the college, there were some joints where people could relax and enjoy simple things like chai, Maggi, and cigarettes.

Dehradun had a vibrant, urban atmosphere, brimming with young people attending various renowned schools and universities. The Indian Military Academy cadets, with their disciplined lives and smart, sophisticated uniforms, naturally caught the attention of the local girls. Although Karan had cleared the National Defence Academy (NDA) entrance, he chose a different path; the petroleum sector offered challenges and possibilities that excited him more than the routine life of a soldier.

Weekends were a time for rest, fun, and a mix of activities. Karan and his friends would play outdoor games, engage in late-night online gaming, chat and plan various parties, and occasionally, they'd trek from Dehradun to Mussoorie. The annual techno-management event, Urja, was one of the grand celebrations where students came together. Karan, known for his speech and communication skills, became among his batchmates' most liked persons. He could motivate people around him with jokes and meaningful words concerning college life and potential life paths.

Finally, Tushar approached Karan with a cup of coffee, and the two resumed their conversation about the bustling airport. Karan reminisced about his first year, particularly the fresher's party thrown by the seniors. As a day scholar, Tushar had to leave early that day, but Karan recounted how the party had continued late into the night. The UPES band had performed alongside some professional bands invited by the college. Karan fondly recalled how juniors and seniors danced together, followed by a lively hostel party

The boarding announcement was finally made, and everyone moved to form a queue. Karan and his friends moved to the boarding gate and finally boarded the plane to take their seats. The flight was fully booked, as usually for night flights. As the plane prepared for takeoff, Karan couldn't help but feel a deep sense of gratitude for the entire course of events in his life. All the challenges, friendships, happiness, and sadness had shaped him into who he was. Like many students, he thought of his family and friends who had influenced him and contributed to his success. These memories and words motivated him—they were the building blocks of his achievements.

Karan felt half-giddy as the plane began its descent into Dubai. He was leaving behind his home and everything associated with it, but so many opportunities awaited him. Karan was excited and determined to succeed despite the new and changing environment he was about to face in the Oil and gas sector.

Dubai was calling, and Karan wasn't going to let it down. Sometimes, the future seemed dark and distant, at other times, closer, but he always envisioned a future better than his past. He was willing to fight, claw, and scrap to make the life he had imagined. The journey had only just begun, and Karan was all set to conquer the world with his talent.

Chapter 02:
Engineering College Recollections

It was time for Karan to shift to his international flight, and he was happy to have secured a window seat. The air hostess's help briefly brought him back to his senses, but Karan's mind wandered to his college days again. This reminded him of the joy of being directly recruited from campus and his dreams of working on an offshore jack-up rig. His thoughts turned to his teachers, the ragging he endured, and the friends he made while in the hostel. Finally, an image of his ex-girlfriend, Manisha, surfaced in his mind. Moments with Manisha, a year junior to him, occasionally appeared, bringing a smile to his face.

Karan's second year of college began with the arrival of Manisha, who belonged to the local Pahadi community. She was one of the new admissions at the college in the same branch as Karan—Petroleum Engineering. Manisha was a shy girl with very little interaction with other students, quite studious and attended school only until evening as a day scholar. Hostel fees were high and not affordable for everyone. She lived with her batchmates in the lower part of the mountains. She was from the Pauri District of Garhwal, where her parents stayed. Her father was a local government employee, and her mother was a homemaker. She had one younger brother who lived with her parents and studied at the local college in Pauri. Pretty and aspiring, she rarely communicated with others even thoattempting and final-year boys attempted to win her attention.

At this time, Karan was occupied with ragging the juniors in the same manner he had been ragged by his seniors. One day, while browsing books in the library, he noticed Manisha. For a few moments, his gaze was riveted on her face. He looked up briefly, then glanced down at the book he had been reading, eyed her again, and returned to his book the moment she walked away. He wasn't even certain she was in his branch because most girls did not go for engineering and even those who did rarely chose petroleum engineering. Karan put his juniors to work, gathering all the information they could on Manisha. After discovering she was indeed in his branch, his initial uncertainty faded, knowing that all the boys had their eyes on her.

Karan had a very good friend, Tushar, who was a day scholar and took on the responsibility of marking his proxies. By the second year, Karan had become quite lazy, often sleeping through the day and waking up only because of his friends. His daily routine was completely supported by the kindness of his roommate and Tushar, who helped him from morning until he closed his eyes at night. It wasn't just Karan; most of his batchmates had also become a bit lazy in pursuing their dreams. Perhaps they realised that life should be a balance between enjoyment and study—something they learned from their seniors who lived by the motto: "ENJOY LIFE AT ITS BEST." Karan's mornings usually went like this: Tushar would call to check if Karan was attending the morning classes and how many proxies he needed to cover for the day. Still asleep, Karan wouldn't respond. Tushar would then call Dsou, Karan's roommate, to ask if Karan had any plans to attend classes. Dsou would try to wake Karan, hoping to hear that he planned to attend, but as always, Karan would disappoint him, saying he would skip class and asking Dsou to convey to Tushar to mark his proxies. Karan would then drift back to sleep while Dsou relayed the message to Tushar.

During lunch, Dsou would wake Karan again to ask whether he wanted lunch. Karan would then ask what was on the menu and inquire if Dsou could pop into the mess. Dsou would leave for lunch, eat, and return to tell Karan what was available. Karan would then ask Dsou to bring food to the room. By the time Dsou returned, Karan would be up, wash his face, eat his lunch, and then leave for college. He would then ask Tushar how many classes the proxies covered and how many more would be needed to reach 75% attendance. This routine tended to become a daily ritual for Karan: classes until evening, then back to the mess for snacks, more online games, gossiping, and speech-making at the Maggi points. Like in other engineering colleges, there were toppers who sat in the front rows, listening carefully to the professors and writing everything down, whether relevant or not.

Karan wasn't on the topper list, but he was enjoying his education. The toppers used to take notes on everything the professors said and duplicated the same in the exams. The professors liked this because they didn't have to do extra work reading new ideas or different ways of thinking. Karan was different; he understood things from books and explored his own way of writing. Although during exams, he had to rush to make copies of the toppers' notes to secure passing marks, this was what the professors liked.

The second year also saw the addition of Dean's classes, which introduced the first course on Introduction to Petroleum Operations, a tough course that required a lot of resources. As the year progressed, the level of study increased and became more time-consuming for everyone, including Karan. There was hardly any time for ragging the juniors, as there were endless assignments to complete every day. Although there was some liberty to pass on a bit of pressure to the juniors, that only lasted until the fresher's party. Overall, the fun continued.

Manisha had very little time on campus as she was a day scholar, except for classes and the time she spent in the library.

One day, when Karan saw Manisha coming out of class, he followed her until she entered the library. He simply walked up to her, introduced himself as her senior, and initiated a conversation. He didn't attempt to rag her but instead adopted a gentlemanly demeanour. He inquired about her college experience, parents, and even told her he would be there to help if she ever needed it. Manisha found him polite, but she realised that many boys offered the same kind of attention.

In Karan's batch, there were six girls, all of whom were in relationships with two boys whom Karan described as playboys. Many of the guys, including Karan, had no attraction toward the girls in their own batch. There was a saying in Petroleum that all the girls were beautiful, except for one percent in their branch.

On the academic side, Petroleum Engineering was all about oil and gas, also known as black gold in today's world. The curriculum covered topics such as drilling, reservoir management, production, transport, and storage. It also included electrical and mechanical engineering principles, essential for understanding how oil rig apparatus functioned. It was somewhat similar to chemical engineering but required knowledge of fluid mechanics and the science of material flow. Both natural gas and heat transfer were also part of the curriculum. There were eight semesters in the four years. In the first year, Karan did well and secured good marks of 3.17 and 3.25 CGPA in the first two semesters, respectively. The study was tough, and having Manisha's presence nearby made Karan's life a bit easier.

Gradually, Manisha became the centre of Karan's attraction, and he began to develop a strong interest in her. He wanted her to love him back, but he knew it wouldn't be easy. The other boys who were attracted to her had it more accessible, boasting bikes with which to woo her, and she had already been noticed by many. However, the love between Karan and Manisha began to blossom more and more with each passing day.

One day, Karan chanced upon Manisha at the college canteen. Even though he had already eaten lunch, just to stay near her, he ordered another meal. She was seated with her fellow batchmates, giggling as they engaged in a noisy discussion. When Karan introduced himself and tried to talk to her, she was polite but quickly left with her friends. Karan felt a bit embarrassed as there were other juniors around, too. But, as they say, all is fair in love and war. Despite this, their exchange was brief, and all Karan could think about was how he could engage with her again. He realised it wasn't enough just to spend time in her company; he needed to do something to capture her heart.

So, Karan thought about what to do and devoted his efforts to studying while he formulated strategies to pursue her. He realised he had to be patient and plan his actions carefully. One day, as he was leaving class, the dean's lecture was still on his mind, and he met Manisha moving in the opposite direction. A warm 'Good morning' from her was met with a distracted nod and an abrupt sidestep from Karan, who was still lost in thought about the Dean's lecture on petroleum. Manisha appeared surprised by his conduct but continued on her way. Karan regretted missing yet another chance to speak to her and cursed the dean's lecture for distracting him.

Every week, Manisha's schedule was packed with classes and assignments, leaving her with little free time. One evening, as she was leaving for home late in the night after attending the library, she heard some noises in the college's community area. Worried about what was happening, she went near the crowd and saw that Karan was standing in the centre, giving a speech in a very motivational way. He sounded very loud, like a leader. He was an eloquent speaker whose topics included motivation, the fight for rights, and being able to work and attain dreams without being prejudiced. Captivated by his words and fervor, Manisha nodded at him. By the time the crowd clapped for him, she was brought back to reality, but Karan's words stayed with her.

This made her curious, and she began to collect as much information about Karan as she could. She felt like she needed to know more about the man who had such an impact on her. Her first concern was resolved when she learned that Karan came from a good family and had not been in any serious relationship before. Feeling safer, she decided to take the first step and approach him.

Their first deep conversation happened in the library. Karan was occupied with his books when Manisha approached him and introduced herself. Karan was surprised but very happy to meet her.

They started by discussing their curriculum and college, but the conversation soon shifted to other topics. They talked about her family, her hometown in the high hills, and her goals in life. Manisha was particularly delighted by the fact that Karan was genuinely interested in her and treated her with respect. Unlike others who had tried to impress her, Karan didn't put on any airs; he was just being himself.

Karan's hostel life was similar to that of other engineering students. Juniors often approached him for advice on classes and how to secure good marks. They were eager to learn how to deal with different professors and get the best grades, though this became secondary once they reached their second year. Other priorities, like enjoying life with friends and girlfriends under the motto "Hostel life is a once-in-a-lifetime experience," took precedence.

Karan had one roommate, Rahul, who stayed with him for all four years. In their three-bedroom room, Karan had the bed near the window, while Rahul took the bed near the door. The middle bed was initially occupied by Himanshu, who was in Karan's branch, but he moved in with other boys in the second year. Karan and Rahul were close throughout their time together, but their third roommate changed every year. Karan also had a strong friendship with Dsou, one of the most popular characters in the hostel. Dsou was liked by everyone because of his jolly nature. He was a topper throughout the four years but remained very down-to-earth. Dsou took care of most tasks for Karan, who in turn had his own ways of showing appreciation and helping out whenever he could.

Karan was busy with assignments, ragging juniors, and getting them to complete his assignments. After classes, they would head to the Maggi Point, depending on what food was available in the mess. Karan, a non-smoker, would accompany his friends to the Sutta Point, which was probably found near every engineering college. They would gossip about professors, girls, and final-year placements—who got jobs and who didn't. In Karan's college, placements were almost 100% due to the high demand in Petroleum and other energy branches.

Karan wasn't overly concerned about placements; he knew he would do well. He enjoyed his education and life. Karan attended classes primarily to maintain the required attendance to be eligible for exams and only studied seriously before exams. Once the semester dates were announced, he would finally open his books and rush to get copies of the toppers' notes. He was a familiar face at the Xerox copy shop in the basement of the college. As exams approached, Karan's visits to the Xerox shop increased exponentially. But in the end, he always managed to secure more than average marks.

As days went by, Karan and Manisha grew closer. They would talk in the library and college arena, sometimes eat together at the canteen or a restaurant, and occasionally walk to their respective classes together. Others noticed the change in Karan, especially his friends. He became more cheerful and stable and seemed to have a new purpose in life. Manisha also experienced new feelings she hadn't felt before. Despite their tight schedules and busy lives, they always found time for each other, drawing comfort and solace from their blossoming friendship in the deep valley of Dehradun.

One evening, Karan found the courage to ask for a more serious date. He proposed that they go on a tour of Mussoorie, the 'Queen of the Hills.' Manisha felt tempted and accepted. They spent the day walking around the beautiful town, discussing their dreams as individuals and as a couple.

As night fell on the hills, a wave of emotions surged through Karan. He knew this was the moment he had been preparing for all these years. Almost as if coming out of a trance, he took a deep breath and confessed his feelings to Manisha. He told her about his love, his admiration for her strength and intelligence, and how beautiful she was. He described how she had become an part of his life and how he envisioned a future together. Manisha listened, her heart pounding in her chest. When he finished, she looked up, tears in her eyes, and said she felt the same way.

From that day forward, Karan and Manisha became inseparable. They stood by each other during the challenges of college life, sharing both the joys and the burdens. Their bond grew stronger with each passing day as they learned to respect and understand one another.

In the second and third years, students were required to undergo vocational training. For his second year of training, Karan joined ONGC in Mumbai. He contacted his uncle, who was posted at Vasundhara Bhawan in Bandra East, ONGC. He was excited to get his first vocational training with ONGC, and for this, Karan boarded a plane to reach Mumbai for the first time. His experience was positive. He completed his training on the comparative analysis of gas compressors at the Uran Plant and Heera Neelam Platform. He also explored the suburbs of Mumbai for leisure. The best part was that he took Manisha with him. It was a good opportunity for Manisha, too, as she gained valuable industrial experience after completing her first year. Karan also introduced Manisha to his uncle, who worked at ONGC, and they had dinner with his family. After the official hours of training, Karan and Manisha explored Mumbai, spending time at Marine Drive, the "Queen's Necklace."

They visited Alibaug and Chowpatty to explore and enjoy the fresh vibes of Mumbai, along with Maratha food and culture. The trip was memorable for Karan, especially since it was his first experience with professional training at such a young age. Karan stayed in a PG in Bandra, which made it easy to access the ONGC office. Later, he was sent to the Uran plant to analyse the performance of existing compressors and assess the need for new ones. Coincidentally, another trainee assigned to the same project was from Dehradun and was pursuing engineering at the Dehradun Institute of Technology. The vocational training lasted for 45 days, which Karan completed successfully. After all the hard work, he returned to his home in Lucknow before finally going back to Dehradun.

Karan and Manisha were a well-liked couple, and they were appreciated and loved by everyone. They were both calm and had a high level of respect and trust for each other.

Manisha took on additional responsibilities when it came to Karan. As a day scholar, she would sometimes cook and bring food that catered to his tastes and requests. She was a hardworking girl, like many other Pahadi girls, and she would wait for Karan's arrival at lunch, no matter how late it was. She managed her time and classes according to Karan's schedule. Karan had his own way of showing his love for Manisha—caring for her at any time, helping her prepare for exams, taking her shopping and carrying her bags, showing her new places in Dehradun, making her laugh, and most importantly, lifting her spirits after a quick argument. Manisha had a deep trust in Karan. She felt very secure with him, second only to her parents. She believed that Karan would stand by her through all situations, good or bad, and couldn't imagine her life without him.

Both of them used to fight, but Karan remained calm and listened to Manisha silently. Both were honest in their relationship. Karan often took Manisha on serene trips uphill, where they cherished their time together. During college, Manisha sought every opportunity to be with Karan, confiding in him about her life, her friends, and her concerns. Karan's maturity shone through in these moments as he calmly addressed her complaints, always offering thoughtful and peaceful resolutions.

Manisha rented a new house and started living alone, as in the last house, it was shared with other girls, and boys were not allowed. Slowly, Karan started spending his weekends at Manisha's house. They cooked together, watched television, played cards, and helped each other with their assignments. At times, they went on trips, mostly following the trails from Dehradun to Mussoorie. Karan was less indulgent with Manisha's batchmates; first, because he didn't have time, and second, because he was senior to them, so he maintained a distance and dignity, and Manisha understood and respected Karan's thoughts. Manisha was more social than Karan in every way; she celebrated all the festivals and made sure that Karan also enjoyed them.

Manisha was always concerned about Karan's daily routine, as Karan was mature but a bit careless with his personal things. Manisha used to manage his clothes and daily needs, more than anything else. Life was going well as Karan started to get busier in his career, but he was always concerned about Manisha.

Karan's parents were aware of their relationship and showed their acceptance in a touching gesture, gifting Manisha a necklace as a symbol of welcoming her into the family.

For the third-year training, Karan chose Assor in the Raniganj block near Asansol, Kolkata, this time without Manisha. Karan was thus able to get a feel for the Bengali culture and gain an actual view of how drilling operations occurred in such regions. This was his first interaction with real-life experience. This training was for two months, and he, along with one batchmate, was recruited for this training program. They took a PG in Bidhan Nagar near the Assor offices. Every day, there was a pickup going to a site that was 70-80 km from the Assor office in some remote area of Bengal. Life was very different in Bengal and full of old traditions. Their basic and favourite food was fish and rice, which was available almost everywhere at an affordable price. As a vegetarian, Karan struggled to find suitable food, while his friend, a passionate meat lover, relished the local cuisine. However, Karan remained focused, reminding himself that his purpose was to learn and gain experience, not seek culinary delights. Every day, they both went to the site where Assor had taken a large block of 500 km² of CBM Block, Coal Bed Methane. They reported to Mr. Aswal, who was in charge and Project Head of Assor for that particular block. He was an ex-ONGC employee. They were assigned a project to make a report on the drilling, production, and completion of a typical exploratory drilling well. They had to wake up early in the morning and get ready to rush to the Assor office to pick up the site vehicle. Their breakfast depended on availability at the site, which was sometimes nonexistent. As Assor was the developer of the CBM project, they had hired other companies, including BJ, to do cementing and completion jobs. Assor had a 1500Hp CABOT land rig and also two smaller 750 HP truck-mounted rigs working at different sites to drill the well. The Coal Bed Methane well is not so deep, only 2000 ft to 3000 ft maximum. While drilling, you have to take care of waterlogging, as these coal seams are flooded with water below the surface, and while drilling, you could hit the aquifers, which could cause water flooding. You have to drill carefully near the coal seam, as Coal Bed Methane is fragile rock; drilling too fast could lead to a blowout, so you have to be cautious at all times while drilling.

The company also hired directional drilling services from Dana Drilling, and they were responsible for directionally drilling and diverting the well at an angle as per the agreed dogleg. Dogleg refers to the intentional deviation in the well's trajectory, measured per foot or meter, to effectively reach the coal seam zone. Wells are not drilled vertically; they are always inclined and directional; hence, the true vertical depth (TVD) and measured depth (MD) are two different parameters used to define the well depth. The coal seam zone has a large surface area and contains a lot of methane gas on the surface. Drilling is not easy for any well, whether it's a CBM well or an oil & gas well. It always carries the risk of encountering trapped gases beneath the subsurface, which can potentially cause a blowout at any depth. Some wells are self-flowing, and for some, you have to stimulate and push the gas via a pump or compressors. There are always abnormal pressure encounters while drilling the well; hence, a blowout preventer is installed as a safety measure. In the past, many incidents occurred at ONGC sites where a well-caught fire while drilling; the crew was casual and went to lunch while drilling, and suddenly, there was a kick, causing the whole rig to explode. You have to be very careful while drilling and take extra precautions at all times. In oil & gas, there is a proverb: "Production is a must, and safety is first."

Karan's third vocational training provided him with invaluable experience. Without Manisha by his side, he devoted his evenings to learning from his seniors, enriching his industrial knowledge in ways he hadn't anticipated. Karan did very well in his training and was appreciated by everyone in the Assor Office. Of course, he also received a farewell party from his seniors, which is very rare. Some seniors also gave him gifts as mementoes. Karan shared all of this with Manisha, and she felt proud of him. These are the small things in Karan's life that were grooming him into a mature man. This time, Karan returned as an experienced man or driller who now had sufficient knowledge of drilling.

The third year was almost the same as the second year. With Manisha now part of Karan's life, they experienced the ups and downs typical of any couple. Their weekdays were consumed by college, assignments, and library sessions, while weekends were dedicated to outings together. In the third year, Petroleum students were offered the choice between upstream and downstream. Upstream relates to the drilling of wells onshore and offshore, mainly engaging in the exploration and extraction of crude oil, with jobs generally based on rigs. Downstream is related to the refining of crude oil, with jobs generally based in cities. In the upstream sector, the money is high, and there is a high chance of going abroad, while in the downstream sector, the money is less, but the job is peaceful, usually at a refinery and mostly domestic. There were lots of choices for the upstream sector, and everyone wanted to go offshore to earn good money. To resolve this, the college put a CGPA barrier; those who got a CGPA above 2.8 were qualified to go for the upstream sector. Karan was one of them, and he opted for the upstream sector. His focus was more on working over offshore rigs.

However, as their last year approached, the pressure from academic work and their dreams started affecting them. The workload and travel schedule intensified with the progression of projects and internships that Karan was now involved in. Karan had to secure a job for himself during campus interviews. The delivery of projects increased, and he became busier than in the past. Manisha also began to feel insecure and apprehensive about the relationship, and although she gave him her support, she continued to pester him.

Nonetheless, the tension in their relationship increased. At times, Karan was highly competitive while Manisha was rather submissive; Karan's energetic character was in direct opposition to Manisha's more measured temperament. They quarrelled and made mistakes, and the pressure of their approaching careers strained their relationship. They agreed to stay friends, which was hard for both of them to accept, but they knew it was the best thing to do. Manisha had feelings of affection for Karan and remained tender toward him, although they decided to part ways in terms of career and study.

It was heartfelt for both Manisha and Karan. Karan was completely occupied with his final year assignments, but Manisha still carried the hope of reunion. Her behaviour toward Karan had not changed much. She still tried her best to spend time with him and still cared for him, but there was a change in Karan. Finally, Karan got selected by Aman Offshore Singapore PTE Limited, along with 4 of his batchmates. Manisha was overwhelmed to hear the news and hoped that everything would be alright now. Aman Singapore PTE Limited was a branch of Aman Offshore in India, headquartered in Chennai. Karan learned that the company required him to join the offshore rig in Dubai, UAE, directly for his training program. Karan was so happy with this, but Manisha was not. Karan threw a job party at the Dehradun Club, and as usual, everything was managed by Manisha. She booked the venue at the hotel and invited Karan's friends, her seniors, and her batchmates. The party was lavish and attended by Karan's parents as well.

The time for farewell arrived as Karan prepared to report to the rig. Saying goodbye to a friend of four years was an emotional moment for everyone. It is said that you live your life only once, and that is your college life. Although friends promise that they will meet again, it doesn't happen, and if it does, it is very rare. The same was true for Karan; he had to say goodbye to his college, to his friend Dsoo, who had been his roommate for four years, to his professors, and most importantly, to Manisha, who had one more year to complete her engineering. After college, people get busy with their lives, and societal pressure makes them different. College life is something when you don't have the pressure to earn, when you don't have family pressure, and all the time, you are surrounded by your friends; you can laugh freely and not be bound by societal customs.

Manisha was not ready, of course; Karan was someone with whom she had spent her precious three years, and now it was time to leave. Manisha was busy packing and buying some important things. All the time, she was thinking about how the next year would be. Everything in college would remind her of Karan, but she had to go through this. Their relationship was over, but Karan was still in her heart. It was not easy for Karan to leave Manisha either, but life goes on. Karan got busy managing paperwork with the company for his visa and all.

These memories revisited Karan's mind as he sat on the plane, waiting for the culmination of the journey to Dubai. The captain's announcement over the speaker brought him back from his reverie. He felt a combination of new feelings, inhibition, and thrill, but the lights of Dubai reassured him.

Hearing the captain's voice that the plane was proceeding for a landing in Dubai brought Karan back to reality. The pilot informed the passengers about the temperature outside the cockpit, the altitude, and the flight speed. On hearing this, the air hostesses got up from their seats and started to pick up objects that passengers had left behind during the flight. Tushar started sharing dreams for their upcoming life, but Karan's eyes were glued to the windows, admiring the breathtaking scenery and the brilliant lights illuminating Dubai. They were a bit afraid as it was a new country to them, and they had heard of the strict laws in Dubai, yet at the same time, there was enthusiasm for having a new experience. Rishab, Harshit, and Shahill were also very excited to see Dubai; they were sitting together and eagerly waiting for the plane to land.

Chapter 03:
Life at Offshore

Despite the turbulence, the plane managed one of the smoother landings typical of Air India—a minor victory for the airline. As the aircraft came to a halt and touched the ground on the runway, the door of the aircraft opened. This was a standard practice where passengers in the business class were allowed to leave the plane first before those in the economy class. Karan and his friends joined the queue, which snaked through a long passageway and opened into a large room. They joined the immigration line, but after a while, they realised they had to go for an eye test because it was their first time in Dubai. They rejoined the queue for the eye scan, which was still manageable at that time.

Dubai Terminal 1 was a major airport, and people from different parts of the world travelled to and from the airport. This was an international city for many mega investors, especially in the oil and gas industry, where several firms had head offices. Karan observed the rich cultural diversity around him—people of various skin tones, from Chinese and Japanese to Eastern Europeans, all converging in this global hub. There was confidence in Tushar's stride as he guided everyone through the airport. At last, they got to the immigration line and had to wait for their turn. Almost similar questions were asked of each of them: What type of activities and accommodation details did one want to pursue during the visit? They had over-rehearsed the answers that HR had fed them to the extent that they could recite them without a second thought. It was amusing to observe that the hall was bustling with Arab guests, many of whom stood tall with their majestic beards, exuding an air of grace and tradition. He also observed that they looked quite distinct from other Indian Muslims; they were very helpful, too. Signboards were everywhere, so if one followed them correctly, one could quickly check out from the airport. The airport was big and glittering from all the corners. A pleasant fragrance wafted through the air throughout.

After crossing immigration, they quickly proceeded to the conveyor belt, where they picked up their luggage. Since Shahil had international roaming, he called the company HR and enquired about the next course of action. HR informed them to get out and search for a man who was holding a sign with the firm's name on it. Before leaving, they exchanged some of their cash into local currency, following HR's advice to carry at least $500 each.

Tushar saw the man with the sign, and they followed him to the parking bay. He informed them of their work assignment to go to an offshore rig in Sharjah. They were a bit surprised as the expectation was to stay in Dubai. They first assumed it would take a long time because Dubai and Sharjah were far apart, but to their surprise, it was not. It was like Delhi-Gurgaon. They all looked out of the windows and observed that all the business establishments seemed to be closed because it was approximately 11 PM. Several shops were still open, and youthful Arabs were seen moving around the stalls.

They arrived at the port and observed that several longships were docked there. They last observed the large structure when the car came to a halt. There it was—an Offshore Jack-Up Rig! An engineering marvel, big, giant, and standing tall. It was far more impressive in person than any photo or media portrayal had ever captured. Everyone got out of the car with their luggage and climbed through a ladder, finding themselves standing on the top part of the vessel, the decking zone. Once they arrived, they met with the safety officer of the rig, who took them to the helicopter briefing room. He introduced himself and asked everyone to introduce themselves, too. He explained the safety process on the rig: Follow the signboard and walk on the walkway only. He also instructed us to report if we noticed anything unsafe. Lastly, he introduced them to evacuation procedures that they should observe in the event of an emergency and their muster cards, which were to be placed at the muster station. The safety officer led them to the muster station and requested they key in their cards. Being at the lifeboat, they had to report in case of an emergency at what was known as the muster station. Tushar and Karan shared the same muster station, and so did Shahil, Rishab, and Harshit; theirs was at the port side.

They were provided a sleeping place with two bunk beds and a washroom shared by two other rooms. That is, four people had to share one washroom. A safety officer guided them to their rooms, unpacked their bags to get their night things, and slipped them into bed.

They awoke around 9 AM the next morning, ready to begin their day with a meeting with the safety officer. He directed them to have breakfast and then head to the Offshore Installation Manager's office. They had to ask some personnel for directions, and they were finally able to get to the mess on the first floor, which they called the galley on the rig. Breakfast was a lavish spread, reminiscent of a five-star hotel, offering a sumptuous and healthy start to the day. After eating, they quickly ran to the OIM's office on the 3rd floor.

The OIM started by introducing himself, then invited each of them to share their backgrounds, creating an atmosphere of mutual respect and professionalism. He explained that the rig was divided into two sections: the drilling team, led by the toolpusher, and the deck crew, which the barge master leads. Both sections were under the supervision of the OIM. He emphasised the need to follow the rig rules and safety policies strictly. He also informed them that their shift would be from 6 in the morning to 6 in the evening since the rig was idle and on standby. As he got a call from the base, he directed them to go to the radio room. The OIM also mentioned that they were highly late for breakfast today, between 5 to 7 in the morning.

After analysing the events, they decided to get to the radio room located on the fourth floor, the top floor of the rig. As for the fire and safety plan, each floor had one. The radio officer was a rather relaxed individual who took their introductions and made them fill out a sheet of special paper listing the contact numbers of individuals. All five were added to the personal crew onboard list. He explained that they could speak with their loved ones for three minutes a week using satellite telephones. He was a tiny bit jolly and handled many tasks, such as being in charge of the chopper landing, assisting in the offloading and backloading of the supply vessel, and occasionally being involved in crane operations.

He also informed them that they could call home at any time in case of an emergency and recharge their internet calling card. He then directed them to the safety office, which he said was on the 2nd floor.

They quickly ran to the second floor and met the safety officer, who was typing on the computer, maybe making the daily safety sheet. He greeted them and spoke to them for nearly an hour on safety, explaining the rig and emphasising the point that every man must know the safety rules on the rig. While many of these protocols perhaps sounded familiar to them, going through them was a different experience altogether. After the detailed briefing about the hot and cold work permit, lock and tag, and the need for PPE on the deck of a rig, it was time for the physical exploration of the rig.

Their eyes had been anticipating this opportunity for four years just to have a glimpse of an offshore rig. He then led them to the material room, where they were issued helmets, glasses, gloves, boots, and coveralls. They proceeded to the ground floor to the changing room, got their belongings from the lockers, and changed into their gear. Venturing out from the accommodation area to the deck, they saw drill bits, three big overhead pedestal cranes, and the drilling section at the end. It was fairly large, and the cantilever area of the first floor was immediately below the drilling floor. They got to the drilling area and saw that the drawworks were used to lift and lower the pipes. This was a manual rig, meaning that rotation was generated by a rotary table, unlike cyber rigs, where a top drive system handles rotation. Other equipment included the iron roughneck used to make joints on the pipes, tongs used to open/close joints on the pipes, and a bridge racker used to stack the drill pipes on. On the drill floor, there was a structure in the form of a trapezium with a total height of 160 feet, necessary for the making of three joints of drill pipe.

They observed the drilling area and the complete deck area and then were introduced to the electrical room, where six Caterpillar diesel generators were installed, and the mechanical room was full of tools and machinery. All of these were on the basement floor, beside the mud pump room. Besides the mud pump room, there was a mud pit room. Lastly, they visited the entire accommodation section, which occupied four floors. The ground floor consisted of changing rooms, a cafeteria, offices/meeting rooms, and washrooms. The first floor had the galley and quarters for the catering team. There were accommodation rooms, an entertainment room, and a prayer room on the second floor. The third floor contained the OIM's office, some senior crew quarters, customer representative offices, and a gym. The fourth floor was occupied by the radio office and the barge master's office, where sea conditions and crew transfer took place.

Gradually, they adapted to the 6 AM to 6 PM shifts, finding a rhythm in the demanding routine of rig life. At first, they had a very tight timetable, but eventually, they began to get accustomed to it. Each of the crew members was polite and helpful, particularly Gurpreet, a floor man who liked to talk and introduced them to the team. He used to take Karan, Tushar, and others for beer and dinner at the seamen's club after their working hours, making them comfortable and relaxed.

They learned that life on the rig was not as harsh as they expected because the rig was idle and awaiting repairs—a fortunate break for newcomers. Gurpreet said the reason for the rig being on standby was that one of its legs had broken during a drilling operation in Qatar.

A week later, Karan and his friends received an eagerly awaited email instructing them to proceed to different rigs and begin the true test of their skills. Tushar had to join Rig DD8, Rishab Aman 8, Karan DD4, Shahil DD2, and Harshit Aman 6. This news brought a mix of anxiety and anticipation as they understood that they were entering the real tests of their chosen professions.

Decision-making regarding their new assignments became a crucial point for all. Everyone regrouped in the living room, recalling the moments they had shared and the bonds, the friendshop they had formed during that week. They were to go to other rigs, and the fellowship they had developed was to be challenged since they were no longer in the same environment.

Karan realised that it would be different from the standby rig, where they had been focused for the past week. The real work would begin soon, and he looked forward to it with added zest and hope of excelling in the job according to his expectations. He had meticulously prepared through training sessions, safety briefings, and hands-on practice, all leading up to this pivotal moment. Anticipation and determination were his two companions when packing his belongings before leaving for a new assignment.

Before they headed their separate ways, Gurpreet called them together for the final time. He encouraged them to remember the safety procedures, the value of collaboration, and the determination to finish the task. Embracing the rough energy with camaraderie, he offered sage words before the shift began: "Remember, the rig is like your second home; treat your second home well, and it will return the favour. Stay safe out there, work hard, and look out for each other."

Karan was provided with a neat, small, but comfortable cabin that he would share with another crew member. He then conveniently settled in, unpacked his luggage, and got comfortable. The cabin had some simple furniture, such as a bed and bedside table, a small desk, and some boxes for storage. It was a long way from home, but Karan was prepared to go with the rough life out there as much as he wanted to be comfortable back home.

Karan's first day on the rig began with a thorough briefing designed to acquaint them with the crucial safety measures that governed life offshore. The safety officer then emphasised the need to follow safety measures and oriented the new recruits on the safety measures aboard the rig. Karan listened patiently, his eyes wide open, as he realised that in times of disaster, these procedures could mean the difference between life and death.

The next morning, Karan and his batchmates had not yet gotten into the rhythm of the rig's schedule and, consequently, failed to attend the morning briefing on board. This made the OIM rather unhappy, and he scolded them severely. It was a reminder of the strictness of the environment they had to face daily. Karan wanted to improve this lax conduct, which is why he decided to wake up earlier and pay more attention.

They went to their training sessions where they learned many things that dealt with the operations of the offshore rigs. They participated in learning about rig technicalities such as drilling methods, equipment care, and risk control measures. The sessions were highly charged, and Karan found them interesting. He was particularly motivated to put theory into practice, as he was with other things.

After a few days at the appropriate location, Karan got used to life on Rig DD4. He got out of bed when it was still dark, had a meal, and proceeded to his duty post. He also realised the value of working in a team and reporting, as each operation had to be done with the help of other personnel. Some of the positive aspects noted by the participants included strong bonds among them, to the extent of supporting each other at work and in rig life.

Weeks later, Karan's confidence began to build up gradually as the months passed. He was able to master himself in his assigned responsibilities and even earned the esteem of fellow subordinates.

Through his experiences, Karan learned one of the most valuable lessons of all—flexibility, the key to thriving in the unpredictable world of offshore drilling. It was a dynamic environment where there were so many underlying factors affecting it, and he had to be ready for anything at any time. Regardless of whether it was a shift in the climate or an issue with the equipment that could have been provoked by anything—be it global warming or mechanical failure—he had to always learn how to improvise quickly.

Looking back at everything that had happened over time, Karan felt like he had indeed come a long way from the University of Petroleum and Energy Studies. Looking at the past, he saw the problems, the camaraderie, the uncertainty, and the achievements that led him to become the man that he is now. Every encounter on Rig DD4 had been earned through merit, each one laying a solid foundation for his career in the oil and gas industry.

It was the time when he learned and underwent challenging moments that would shape him in the Oil & Gas sector towards the realisation of his dreams. When Dubai called, Karan eagerly answered, embracing the opportunity to be part of a dynamic organisation where the work was as vibrant and fast-paced as the city itself.

By now, they had a complete idea that life on an offshore rig was not easy—drilling for black oil from the ground was not simple. This also meant that every day began in the morning without any regard for feeling ill or well. When they were issued transfer letters to new operational rigs, they all got ready to leave behind their first rig, Aman 7. The final scene between Karan and Tushar was touching—they had been good friends for four years and had worked in the same company, but now they had to part ways and look for a new job.

Both Tushar and Rishab left on the same day for their rigs. The next turn was for Karan and Harshit. Karan packed his gear and decided to spend his remaining night at the helideck, observing the movement of the ships. The following day, a car was sent to take him from the rig, and he was later dropped off at the airport.

At the airport, Karan met his new companions: Punjab-born Hardeep, Goa-born Vishal, a Delhi boy named Arun, the young assistant driller, the new OIM from Orissa, Mr Mehra, and the toolpusher, Sakun Kumar from Uttarakhand. They all extended their hands to Karan, and he did the same in return. The crew was prepared to travel to the Persian Gulf, where the rig was located at that time. It was a 45-minute flight from Dubai to Kish Island in Iran. Initially, thinking about Iran made Karan a bit uncomfortable, but everyone assured him that everything was fine and safe. Tushar and Rishab had also gone to Iran but were at a different installation, Bushehr.

They collected their boarding passes for the 45-minute flight and seated themselves anywhere they could find space. A Persian air hostess came; she was very beautiful, but she was almost dressed from head to toe in veils. They served juices and cashews, which were easy to exhaust within the short period of the flight. They eventually reached the island of Kish, which was described as being "desolate." A man from the area took their passports and got them through immigration without having to stand in a big line.

They got out of the airport and went to the Hotel Flamingo, an artificial structure designed in Persian architecture. A local agent informed them it was time to get ready to leave at 9:00 AM for a boat ride from Kish to the rig. They went to their separate rooms, changed clothes, and later reunited at the restaurant for lunch. Karan was a vegetarian, and this was not easy, but he was able to order rice and daal. In the restaurant, daal is referred to as soup. At lunch, they talked about the rig operations and later agreed to go to the beach in the evening.

At the beach and shopping malls, they observed families, mainly women with their children, being accompanied by their husbands, some of whom were smoking. Later on, Karan inquired if they could locate a bar similar to the one in Dubai, only to be informed that alcohol consumption was prohibited in Iran and was considered a punishable offense.

They went back to the hotel. At night, everybody had to come to the restaurant, but Karan refused to come. He said to one of his crew members that he was not feeling like eating. Perhaps he was missing his friends. Kish Island was a very peaceful place where you could hear your own breathing. Everything was so quiet that Karan felt like he had travelled two centuries back.

In the morning, they all woke up and prepared for the rig as they were set for departure. The agent came with two cars, which drove them to the port. He checked on them for a long time, and finally, they waited for the boat. When it arrived, people quickly boarded and sat down, all of which surprised Karan with so much hurry. Once seated, they reclined, took covers, and slept. Karan was quite amused at why people were in such a hurry, only to realize soon that the crew boat, which was moving at the rate of 14 knots, kept rising and falling, causing weightlessness and nausea. Karan started feeling dizzy nauseated, and vomited several times before he lay down and slept. An able seaman handed him some vomiting pills, which provided relief.

A new country, a foreign land, a Persian nation—all of it was too swift for Karan's perception. Dehradun to Delhi to Dubai to Iran; land, air, and now sea. He finally was able to notice the lights of the rig and felt a little better, reassured that they had not moved. The crew got up and looked into Karan's condition. Karan saw the rig, a giant steel structure with three framed legs, positioned in the centre of the sea. As soon as the crew boat got close to the rig, the deck, which was approximately 15 meters above the sea, lowered a personnel basket to facilitate the crew change. Tasks were delegated to the following crews by the previous crews.

Karan climbed into the personnel basket, which then lifted him to the radio room floor, 5 meters above the deck. He already had an idea about the rig, but working at sea was unfamiliar to him. The same procedures followed: the new crew members underwent the safety drill and also obtained their muster station cards, which they inserted into the port or starboard holders. They then proceeded to go to their respective rooms.

Karan felt the heat and decided that he had to embrace change and become capable of accommodating all the changes that he had encountered since he had gotten a chance to work for Vision Limited, so he got into his room and slept. This situation left him lonely, and the new environment produced psychological consequences for him. He noticed that the new crew went first to the changing room and then directly to the deck to work, which was rather unusual for him. In the case of crew succession, there was a 12-hour shift difference, which was to be made good by the relieving and joining crew.

The next morning, like at Aman 7, Karan had a wake-up call at 5 AM, took his breakfast, and at 6 AM, reported to the OIM's office. After Karan went through the training program of the OIM, he was posted to serve one hitch of 42 days in the deck department. He was directed to go to the material man's office and collect new PPE, then proceed to the barge master. Upon tearing off his PPE, Karan went to the barge master and was assigned the cleaning of the chemical compartment as the first task. This was surprising to Karan, who expected that with his qualification in petroleum engineering, he would not be doing such basic tasks. After some harsh words were exchanged with the barge master, he received a diplomatically worded warning letter. Karan soon realised that these menial tasks were an essential part of his training, providing him with a hands-on understanding of the equipment and operations.

For the next few days, Karan was given jobs such as greasing equipment, painting, chipping, and buffering. These tasks were slightly more complex, although physical labour was still involved in this occupation. The initial period was very tough for Karan; the psychological strain of isolation and tasks took a significant toll on him.". As the sea surrounded them, at times, they could see passing ships, dolphins, fishing boats, or supply boats that brought food containers and other equipment; these little things gave Karan happiness. Karan took a full tour of the rig in two days. By now, he was almost aware of all the equipment on the rig. Karan's rig was a cyber amphion jack-up, an imposing steel giant supported by three massive legs. These legs were made of solid steel columns and attached rack and pinion joints, which helped move the legs up and down. The hull was actually a water-tight barge that floated on the water's surface. When the rig reached the work site, the crew jacked the legs downward through the water and into the sea floor (or onto the sea floor with mat-supported jack-ups). This anchored the rig and held the hull well above the waves. To move the legs up and down, they were connected with heavy induction motors placed in the hull of the rig. Offshore rigs were like ships but with an additional part for the drilling floor, and here, the deck was a bit more modified to make maximum space for the drilling equipment, mud chemicals, and crane operations. The average weight of a jack-up rig ranged between 30-35 thousand tons. Jack-up rigs were mainly designed to work in shallow water up to 300 or 350 ft water depth. If deeper water drilling was needed, then floaters, semi-submersible rigs, or drillships were used. A jack-up rig was a floating-type barge fitted with long support legs that could be raised or lowered.

Compared to city or office life, life on the rig was very different, and yet this place was home to all of them. Every day, they had their work, a set number of hours, and no layaway. The shift required 12 hours of duty and an additional two to three hours for paperwork, training, or reading operations. Such physical and mental pressure did not cease day or night, during weeks, months, and sometimes, years. The third **challenge—**the psychological impact of the sea—was the most difficult; no matter which way Karan turned, there was only water. This was perhaps why the lower crew, who were mostly illiterate but strong in physical tasks, engaged mostly in bantering, and their major topic of discussion seemed to be sex as a form of relief.

However, Karan came to learn several things about drilling and other supportive positions. He socialized with everybody with the intention of knowing what their positions entailed. The crew members were friendly, and even though things were tough in the industry, they supported each other. After some weeks, Karan adjusted to the rig's schedule to some extent. He began to appreciate the small comforts on the rig—steaming cups of black coffee, refreshing green tea, and an assortment of biscuits, salads, and pickles that were available at all hours. The food was even quite decent, with options to suit vegetarian as well as non-vegetarian palates. These meals were grouped into breakfast, lunch, dinner, and mid-morning/mid-afternoon snacking to sustain and nourish the crew. In essence, the rig's discipline required more hours of working with less sleep since the operations ran around the clock. Not even lunch or dinner could be attended without a swap in the position of responsibilities.

During his first hitch, he witnessed many drilling and rig operations, some of which he actually got to be involved in. He gained knowledge in handling and operating big machines and how much precaution and care were vital in every single operation. The education Karan received on the rig was invaluable, providing a solid foundation for his future career in the oil and gas industry. During his training on deck, he learned many things, like making different types of knots, different types of lifting gears, sometimes going to the crane and operating it, and crane parts like the main block for heavy loads, the auxiliary block for lighter loads, and putting on a safety belt while working at height. He also became an expert in making hot permits and cold permits as per the work requirements and maintaining log books.

During the landing of a helicopter, which was a critical operation, Karan had the opportunity to act as a fire watch. He would wear a fire suit and stand near the fire pump so that, in case there was a fire in the helicopter, he could spray water. When there was a boat, the responsibility was given to Karan for the safe off-loading of drilling equipment from the boat to the rig and back-loading from the rig to the boat if necessary. This operation was not easy; first, you had to consider the wind to determine whether this operation was possible or not. If yes, then you had to decide which way to call the boat—either port side or starboard side.

Generally, the sea was very rough, and because of heave and sway, the boat moved up and down a lot. The lift could collide with the deck of the boat while being lifted by the crane, potentially damaging the deck of the boat and sinking the boat.

Almost all operations on the rigs were very critical because of the difficult weather conditions. Strong winds, high waves, and other challenges were constant. There was safety equipment available: lifeboats for sufficient people—three, with two on the port side and one on the starboard side—and six liferafts, three on each side, starboard and port side. A lifeboat or liferaft was a small, rigid, or inflatable boat carried for emergency evacuation in the event of a disaster aboard a ship. There were also eight buoys in case anybody went overboard. Karan also mixed a lot to prepare the mud, as the mud was required to maintain the counter pressure on the formation while drilling. The most important job on the floor was to maintain the stability of the rig, which occurred during rig move time and during rig installation at the platform. Karan witnessed this operation only during his first hitch. His rig had completed a well, and now they had to move to a new location, and moving to a new location required a lot of preparation. Rig moves were a very critical operation; in the past, many rigs had sunk because proper procedures were not followed. This was a very common accident in the offshore industry, so you had to be very alert during rig move operations. Karan also had not studied this before and had no idea. Karan was informed that they were moving the rig to a new location 25 nautical miles from the present location in the same field of South Pars.

Karan had never heard of such operations before, but everyone started to work very fast. All the drilling operations ceased completely; all the drilling equipment was stacked, and the drill crew became completely occupied with stacking all the drilling equipment. Karan learned that rig moves were subject to suitable weather and a favourable forecast for the duration of the entire move. Predicted wind speeds should not normally exceed 15 knots, and swell/sea heights should be less than four feet. The deck crew also became busy putting grease on the racks of the legs, and then the barge master began the jack-up operation, which shook the rig completely. It felt as if the rig might fall into the sea. The same jack-up operation continued until the hull was immersed in the seawater.

Karan watched as three powerful tugboats approached the rig. Once they were securely tied to the rig with towing chains, they began the delicate task of towing the massive structure. Upon asking, Karan learned that each tug had a 5000Hp engine and was strong enough to pull the offshore rig. This whole operation was carried out by a rig mover who was an expert in this area. It was a very critical and complex operation. A small mistake could have toppled the rig, and the company could have lost 200 million dollars in assets. In fact, a lot of preparation was required at the new location as well. A seabed survey report and the last coordinates where the rig was picked up and drilled were required to avoid mistakes; a proper plan was prepared in discussion with the rig mover and the tugboat captains.

This was the most critical operation Karan had witnessed in his first hitch, and although there was very little work during the rig move, the main task was to ensure that everything was properly secured and latched. Work intensified threefold once the rig reached the new location, and the deck and drill crews became busy with their respective jobs. Offshore work wasn't like working on land. Every moment, you had to be cautious; one mistake could cost you your life. You were in the middle of the sea, where the water depth was 100 meters.

Finally, it was Karan's turn, marking the completion of his duties and his eagerly anticipated sign-off. He was ready to return home—happy and somewhat relieved, although he would have been glad to put in a few more hours of practice. Time had taken its toll on him; he had worked harder than he thought he would, which led to his desire to take a break. The signing-off process included obtaining a crew list, which felt like getting a ticket to heaven for Karan. He was eager to see land after more than seven weeks on the water.

As the boat arrived to pick them up, Karan cheerfully bid goodbye and departed in the boat to Kish Island. He spent some time in Kish, sleeping, dreaming, and reflecting on what had happened. The following morning, he flew to Dubai and, to celebrate, had a beer party with his crew. The highly paid senior crew members spent lavishly on themselves, going on shopping sprees and purchasing gold, whiskey, and electronic gadgets, among other things. Karan also purchased some whiskey bottles before taking a night flight back to Delhi. When Karan landed in Delhi, he was delighted to enjoy his favourite North Indian food once again. After that, he flew to Lucknow on a domestic flight, where he planned to meet his friends and family and take a rest before starting his next hitch.

Karan's first hitch had been an emotional rollercoaster, full of feelings, difficulties, and valuable lessons to learn. He had transitioned from the familiar comforts of home and university to the uncharted and unpredictable world of the sea. He had faced real-life conflict situations that challenged him physically and psychologically, and, as a result, he had gained deeper understanding and strength. The friends that he had made, the experiences he had shared, and the things that he had been taught would stay with him as he continued his career in the oil and gas industry.

Karan would be proud of the hardships and challenges that he had experienced, and he would feel that he had accomplished something. It wasn't the end of the road yet, but if this was what awaited at the end of the road, then he was ready for it.

Chapter 04:
Base Life & Libya War

After relaxing in Lucknow, Karan received a call from the Human Resources department in Mumbai, informing him about his mandatory Offshore Survival Training—a vital step in advancing his career. He might have been too tired after the previous hitch, but he knew exactly how much he needed this Offshore Survival Training for his career. He decided on the flight date to Mumbai, recalling his time spent in the city during his second-year vocational training.

As Karan arrived in Mumbai, memories of his earlier days in the bustling city flooded back, each corner holding a piece of his past. It was a thriving city that he recognised, and all sorts of memories of the time he had spent there with Manisha flooded his mind. Being a highly paid professional, he booked a room in the hotel beside the Taj at the Gateway of India. The training was to be carried out at the Naval Maritime Academy, and Despite his exhaustion, Karan's determination kept him going, knowing how crucial this training was for his future.

On the first day of training, instead of using his own vehicle, Karan hired a taxi to travel to Cheetah Gate. The instructor was a navy man who demanded discipline and informed them how tight the following days would be. Basic Offshore Survival Training consisted of helicopter underwater escape training, basic first aid, firefighting, and personal survival training. Karan understood the value of learning these skills, as he needed to protect himself and achieve his goals in the offshore environment.

Once, in the middle of what seemed to be a theoretical class where he was daydreaming, Karan glanced around the classroom and, to his delight, saw Manisha's face. Overjoyed, he shouted out her name at the top of his voice, and soon the entire class, including Manisha, was looking at him. The instructor quickly interrupted and asked Karan to focus. Manisha looked at Karan for a moment, then smiled and nodded in acknowledgement.

During the breaks, Karan and Manisha could not wait to meet each other. They discussed their lives, their college days at the University of Petroleum and Energy Studies, and their second-year vocational training in Mumbai. The initial joy of seeing each other after a long time made the training sessions more palatable. Karan felt very motivated, knowing that Manisha was there.

Manisha had joined Reliance, which was based in Mumbai.

Apart from training hours, Karan and Manisha went out to places of interest within Colaba and the rest of Mumbai. They visited the places they loved the most; Alibaug and Marine Drive, among others, were included. They reconnected, revisiting old memories, but Karan couldn't shake the feeling that something fundamental had shifted between them. The first signs of affection were quickly masked by a certain degree of stress, which might have stemmed from their previous experience or their working positions.

Karan realised that although they were good friends, there was some distance between them. Manisha appeared attentive but less engaged, and the conversation, while tender, was not as passionate as before. Still, Karan did not want the time they spent together to be unproductive. They went on weekend trips to the suburbs and tried to revisit the romantic paradise of Lonavala and Pune. They had been in a long-term relationship, and Manisha loved Karan deeply, but it did not work out. Karan knew this, but all of this had happened, and nothing could be changed in the past. Signs of regret could be easily seen on Karan's face at many moments.

Once Karan finished his training, he had to get back to Rig DD4. Though the thought of leaving Manisha again filled him with dread, Karan knew there was no escaping the pull of his responsibilities. He returned to Lucknow to pick up his belongings, proceeded to Delhi, and from there to Dubai, Kish Island, and Rig DD4.

Back on the rig, Karan was thrust into the relentless grind of his daily routine, the intensity of rig life quickly engulfing him once more. Part of his life consisted of 12-hour working shifts on the drilling floor and extra hours doing paperwork. He was transferred to the electrical department, where he not only acquired new experience but also became accustomed to the intensified schedule and the heat of the engines. Contact with the outer world was constrained, which made it impossible for him to maintain contact with Manisha. However, the physical and mental demands did not deter Karan; he needed to work because he understood how important work-related experience was to his career.

The next job assignment given to Karan was on the drilling floor, which involved much more rigorous tasks and required precision and concentration. It was a rigorous technical process, which included the use of heavy tools in the drilling activities. Karan also became acquainted with how to operate the drawworks, which are used to lift and lower the pipes, as well as other equipment, such as the iron roughneck, that helps in making joints in the pipes.

Karan concluded that it was a challenging job, but he found it very fulfilling. He realised that he could learn more about the drilling procedures, safety measures, and cooperation with other members. The relationships were good, and they helped each other when things went bad. His hardworking nature, commitment to the job, and willingness to listen to those around him made them develop respect for him. During his training program, he had to work with every person on the drilling floor. He used to go to the derrickman to support him at around 100 ft high from the drilling floor. Sometimes, he assisted the assistant driller in making the bottom hole assembly, and sometimes, he worked with the floor man in lifting the slip, which was so heavy that it required three people to lift it. The slip was the equipment used to hold the drill string weighing a hundred tons. He also worked with the driller in the dog house to complete the paperwork, so overall, Karan's experience went very well. As a trainee, Karan was well-liked and supported by the crew, who took special care to guide him on the floor. Despite their vigilance, Karan made several mistakes—some of which could have resulted in serious injury or worse—but his teammates were always there to pull him back from the brink. Karan was sometimes sent to a shale shaker and sometimes to a mud pit room to mix chemicals and prepare the mud.

Drilling offshore is a very complex process that requires lots of precision, an understanding of subsurface structures, and the maintenance of safety all the time. Geologists are always on board and keep checking what's coming from the well. It's just like fighting with an enemy whom you don't know. There could be shallow gas, which could cause a blowout, or there could be abnormal pressure in any pay zone. Sometimes, the drilling pipes get stuck in the formation. In that case, you have to do a fishing operation, cut the drill pipe and lift it with the fishing jar. It's also a very expensive process, as whatever tools and equipment are used must have high pressure and high temperature bearing capacity. Nothing small and light works here; each casing pipe weighs around 1 ton. Handling the massive casing pipes, each weighing around a ton, in the tight confines of the rig was no small feat.

The drilling process in shallow water is done with multiple processes, and most commonly, the customer company installs the jacket wherever they need to drill. A jacket is an unmanned steel structure that is set on the seafloor and provides a platform for rigs to drill. A jacket is the lower version of a platform, as jackets are mostly unmanned, and platforms are bigger and have accommodation for the crew. The first process is the rig move, in which a jack-up rig is towed by towing vessels to the platform and set there with the help of towing boats. Once the orientation of the rig is set with the platform, another operation is the lowering of legs, which is called jack down. The jack-up rig's legs are anchored by piles at their base, housed within the spud can—a trapezium-shaped steel structure designed to provide a stable foundation. The piles get inserted into the seabed upon reaching it. The seabed formation is usually very soft, and this whole operation is done very slowly to avoid any type of damage to the legs on the seafloor. It's like a trapezium shape that gives stability to the rig and is filled with water to add weight to the rig so that it can insert more. After that, the barge master of the rig performs ballasting, which means filling the tanks, which are small compartments in the lower section of the rig filled with water to increase the rig's weight and provide stability. After this, the barge master instructs the deck crew to open the bottom plug to flush the seawater from the tanks. By this time, the rig has enough weight inserted into the sea floor and is stable. This whole process is called ballasting; after this, the skidding process starts, involving the movement of the cantilever to the platform, which allows the rig to move toward the platform and position itself over the platform. Once it is done, the skidding process continues for the drilling floor, and as per the well, we set the drilling floor over the top of that.

This whole process takes time, and it is not that easy; every piece of equipment must perform well. Once the drilling floor is set over the well, we use a riser and nipple to reach the seafloor. We insert the conductor casing and follow this by setting the blowout preventer and starting the drilling with the drill pipes. This entire process must be completed in three to four days in the shortest possible time; if something fails or breaks, then it results in direct downtime, meaning no money would be paid to the rig. Drilling offshore is like a continuous running process; you can't halt the operation even for half an hour. Every day, the DPR is prepared in which all the progress made on an hourly basis is recorded, including the number of personnel onboard, man hours spent, and if any lost time incident (LTI) occurred, indicating if anybody was injured, whether minor or major. If yes, then it will be discussed in the upcoming safety meeting. These reports are reviewed in safety meetings and sent to the IADC, which monitors drilling companies and

LTIs, issuing new safety norms based on these insights.

Deepwater rigs are floating rigs, and they generally dig new wells with the help of a temporary guide base, which is lowered into the sea and positioned at the location with the help of CCTV. Once the temporary guide base is set on the seabed, we set the permanent guide base, which ensures drilling at one point only. In deep sea drilling, we set the most important safety equipment, the blowout preventer, at the seabed and operate it with the ROV. Initially, we use a string of conductor casing lowered from the sea level to the seabed and then hammer it down. The next job is to secure the well with the conductor casing, and the size of the conductor is typically 26" or 20", depending on the customer's requirements. After the conductor pipe is hammered into the seabed, it gradually embeds itself deeper with each strike until it is fully secured, ensuring the well's stability.

Working on drilling rigs is a different level of experience. You must be attentive all the time. Offshore rig space is already constrained, and in that environment, everything is stacked in a small space. The drill pipes, casing pipes, tongs, iron roughnecks, and slips all weigh tons. A small hit from this equipment could cause significant damage and, in fact, could make you handicapped—even a small bolt falling from a 100 ft height could tear your helmet and penetrate your head. This type of accident happened multiple times on rigs. Safety is very important. On rigs, there is a saying: you arrived in one piece, and you pray every day that you leave in one piece. Life is tough on offshore rigs; besides the physical job, you have the psychological pressure that you are in the middle of the sea. No matter where you looked, the endless expanse of blue water was all that met your gaze, a constant reminder of your isolation from the rest of the world. There was always the feeling that everything on the planet had finished, and you were left with your teammates at sea. In the early days, it feels good, but after a couple of hitches, it drives you crazy. Living at sea is not easy at all.

After work, and whenever he finished early, Karan sometimes went to the helideck to feel at peace. It was a moment when you could reflect; it was almost like sitting at the beach. Being in the middle of the sea at night, the water looks completely black and scary. There are no boundaries on the helideck, although there is sufficient light available on the rig. You are completely surrounded by the sea, which is 300 ft deep. The waves are high, and if you fall overboard, you don't know where you will end up in the next hour. Yet, it also offers a sense of peace. At night, operations become lighter than during the day. Deck work generally stops, as you can only operate the crane at night if it is very urgent. Helicopters are not allowed to land at night.

Generally, the Persian Sea is a very calm sea, but Karan once faced a tough incident when there was a storm. The wind started to blow at a speed of more than 50 nautical miles per hour. Everyone was scared, and it was the first time that all operations halted, including crane operations. The crane boom was secured so that it would not fall. The gust of wind was so strong that seawater started coming onto the deck. Usually, the deck is 15 meters high from sea level. But the wind was so strong that seawater started coming onto the deck. We all came to the ground floor, and instead of reporting at the muster station, we all put on life jackets and stood under the accommodation area. Everything was shaking, even the legs of the rig. At that time, Karan truly felt the power of nature.

During drilling, the legs of the rig sometimes shake, and you can feel it while sleeping in your bunk bed. Sometimes, it made Karan very uncomfortable and interrupted his sleep in the middle of the night.

There were regular drills almost every week and safety meetings held every week, which were compulsory for everyone to attend. They happened twice so that both shifts could attend. There were two shifts for the crew: one from midnight to noon and another from noon to midnight. There was also onsite training, where instructors came to rigs and gave classes. It used to be the most boring time after work for those who attended classes. Karan completed many onsite trainings like forklift training, log out and tag out training, rigging and slinging training, fire watch training, and others.

Amidst hard sea weather and a scorching sun, Karan felt suffused with a sense of satisfaction. He understood that every day the rig was out at sea brought him a day closer to his dreams of having a high-paying career. The conditions on the drilling floor only encouraged him to press on and overcome whatever odds were in his way. But as the hitch continued, Karan became more confident and did his job more efficiently, to everyone's surprise. The rotation offered him a good grounding for his future career in the Oil & Gas sector.

Despite the hard-working hours and straining responsibilities, Karan often had Manisha in mind. The thought of reuniting with Manisha during his off days became his beacon of hope, driving him to endure the toughest challenges. The relationship they shared, despite the current state of separation, was something that gave him hope.

These experiences on the drilling floor strengthened his knowledge of the oil and gas industry and also equipped him with the skills needed for the many more challenges ahead. He was passionate about his job, and though there was distance and challenges, he was willing to fight for his love life with Manisha as much as for his career.

As soon as Karan was done with his shift on Rig DD4, he couldn't wait to go back to India for his break period. The first thing that came to mind was to meet Manisha. He returned home with some gifts for her and his family, including a gold necklace for Manisha. After staying in Lucknow for a couple of days, he contacted Manisha and let her know that he would be coming to Mumbai shortly.

While they were in Mumbai, they enjoyed each other's company by exploring the city and revisiting some of the places that they had visited before, creating new memories. They travelled to Lonavala and Pune on the outskirts, where they could enjoy a good view of nature and avoid the hustle and bustle of Mumbai. Though they tried to revive their friendship, Karan couldn't escape the feeling that something was lacking between them. The conversations were not as lively as before, and it seemed like something weighed on Manisha's mind.

This pattern of working on the rig and spending his off time with Manisha went on for several months. Every time Karan returned to the rig, he focused on his job and tried to acquire as much knowledge as possible to demonstrate his loyalty to the team. He often visited Mumbai on his off days to be with Manisha despite the distance that was growing between them.

However, the pressure that a long-distance relationship brought and the rigorous work schedule made him realise that he was struggling to balance work and family responsibilities. Still, he tried his best, but distance and different experiences started to create a physical and metaphorical wall between them. The passion that the two once shared diminished as they faced the reality of being in a long-distance relationship, fully aware of their tight working schedules in different cities.

Yearning for stability and aiming to strengthen his relationship with Manisha, Karan, after completing his training in all the departments and feeling that he had learned enough to operate the rig, finally decided to resign from his first job. He left his offshore job and joined a company in Mumbai as a base. He joined Zindal Drilling, which operated a fleet of five offshore jack-up rigs, as the deputy operations manager, where he was responsible for the operation and inspection of several jack-up rigs. This new position enabled him to remain in Mumbai and gave him more time to be with Manisha.

For a while, it seemed as though their relationship had entered a smoother phase, with both Karan and Manisha relishing the ease of being together without the strain of long separations. They enjoyed the fact that it was easy for them to meet without the bothersome interruptions of offshore jobs. They used their weekends for local sightseeing, eating out, and even mapping out future travel dates. However, the change did not proceed as smoothly as Karan had anticipated.

This heightened the awareness of their different ways of life and their cherished priorities. Manisha, who had her own job and friends in Mumbai, was uncomfortable with Karan's intrusion at every stage of her life. There were clear signs of changes in their schedules and tensions that they could not let go of as they had been away from each other for some time.

However, their relationship began to unravel as unresolved issues surfaced, leading to frequent conflicts and a growing emotional distance. Living in the same city was exciting at first, but before they could get used to it, they dealt with old problems and new frustrations. Manisha felt that she was suffocating and unhappy with her life, so she decided to take a pause and pursue her career. She got a chance to get a job in the USA and seized it as she felt it was an opportunity to start anew.

Karan had quit his job with an offshore company and completely overhauled his life for a relationship that was quickly coming to an end. He attempted to persuade her to stay back, but she was already determined not to. The last time they met at Marine Drive, there were a lot of things to be said, but they still needed to be said. It slowly dawned on Karan that no matter how hard you try, everything will not always turn out to be a success where love is concerned. It became apparent that Manisha was no longer there to fill that void in his life, and he had to seek fulfillment elsewhere.

Karan devoted himself to a new position at Zindal that involved overseeing the operations of five jack-up rigs. His job sometimes required travelling to offshore installations for inspections or for resolving troubleshooting issues. He was able to thrive in the position and was soon regarded as a respected member of the team. However, the routine became monotonous, and Karan longed for the thrill and excitement of the offshore job. He also got an opportunity to undergo training on Nuclear Gauges at Bhabha Atomic Research Center in Chembur, Mumbai, which added a lot of value to his professional career. Everything was going well, except he wasn't enjoying his personal life.

At night, Karan used to enjoy Mumbai nightlife, and these things often reminded him of Manisha. He was trying his best to escape from her memories, but sometimes it was very difficult. Karan began immersing himself in work, even on weekends, spending long hours clearing backlogs and trying to fill the void left by Manisha. Nights were spent either with colleagues or alone, battling the emptiness that haunted him. All of Karan's colleagues were married, and that was the reason why they preferred to spend time with their families on weekends. Life in Mumbai without Manisha was quite challenging. Karan was now living in Andheri West but soon moved to Kala Nagar, Bandra East, and then again shifted to Navi Mumbai for a new beginning. He used to travel to work by AC bus, and later, he purchased his first car, which was a Chevrolet Cruze. Karan's new home was in Navi Mumbai; the commute was sometimes exhausting, but more was needed. Karan sometimes sent messages to Manisha to find out more about her new life, and the replies he received were very late and sometimes nonexistent.

There is a proverb: "Never be a prisoner of your past because it was just a lesson and not a life sentence."

To avoid the memories of Manisha, Karan started traveling, and he first visited his rig, which was brought to South Goa Port for dry-docking and inspections. Karan planned to go there and prepare the rig for the next contract. There was some underwater leg inspection required, and Karan scheduled his trip to conduct this successfully.

He was promoted and rose to the position of Operations Manager. Nonetheless, he sought more and was somewhat aggressive toward his coworkers, thus having issues with organisational executives.

Frustrated with the lack of challenge in his current role, Karan embarked on a determined search for a new job that could reignite his passion. He was able to secure an opportunity with Quad Petroleum Company on a land rig in Libya, which he took despite the civil war that had recently occurred in the country. The country was still recovering from the war, and the dangers did not seem very far-fetched. But Karan was determined not to give up this fresh challenge, as he knew that this could prove to be a life-changing point for him.

After a lot of thinking and analyzing, Karan finally agreed to join Quad Petroleum, a company planning its operations in the challenging field of post-civil-war Libya. Memories of Manisha still preyed on his mind, and his disappointment with his work at Zindal added to his yearning for a new job. He quit his job at Zindal and handed over his passport to Quad Petroleum. The latter arranged his visa and prepared him for the trip to Libya.

Nothing went as planned when Karan arrived in Libya. The country, struggling with the consequences of the civil war, was a battleground on which diverse forces conflicted. Italian and French forces were posted all over the area, guarding oil and gas concessions. The oil companies, including the national oil company that had stakes in the country, were forced to pay high premiums to the foreign forces. Karan soon realised that crude oil, also known as the 'black gold,' was the lifeline of all economies.

Karan's drilling site was 300 kilometres north of Libya's capital, Tripoli, which was a very risky area to drill in, with actual gun battles nearby. People's lives were increasingly at risk as the civil war progressed. Promises of job security became null, many firms closed, and even food became scarce. The extreme need for food led people to exchange oil for food. Karan was amazed at the sight of oil tankers being swapped for food, realising that they lacked the basics like food in the region, even though there was plenty of oil.

Working on an onshore land rig was a completely new experience compared to Karan's previous experience on offshore rigs and platforms. The climatic conditions were equally unforgiving, with very high temperatures and perennial dust storms. The rig site, of course, was a high-traffic area with various installations and workers constantly on the move 24/7. Karan had to adjust to the new environment and become an active part of the day-to-day business operations. The good thing was there was ample space to keep equipment and no space constraints like on an offshore jack-up rig with its sea psychological effects.

The work was physically demanding, often requiring Karan to lift heavy equipment and endure gruelling, all-consuming tasks that tested his strength and stamina. He needed to accustom himself to land rig operations, which were quite distinct from those on offshore platforms. Additionally, he gained knowledge about the general factors involved in onshore drilling, such as the type of soil at the drilling site and how to ensure that the rig was anchored firmly. There was also a bond between the crew; they stood by each other, especially during times of adversity.

Every day was tough because he had to fix everything from the mechanical equipment of the rig to other general issues such as the supply and logistics of people. These challenges included exposure to toxic atmospheres, hazardous chemicals, high risk of accidents, long working hours, and more. Karan's past experiences while working on offshore rigs proved beneficial in managing these issues.

He gained first-hand management experience on the land rig by observing how various innovations in drilling technologies and safety measures were employed. Karan also gained more insight into how crucial it was to work as a team and for everyone to convey their ideas to the team to ensure the rig operated smoothly. Yet, he found satisfaction in managing the numerous physical and mental challenges on a day-to-day basis to sustain and even increase the rig's production level.

The Libyans took time to rest and explore new places over the weekends. As noted, Karan and his assistants would go to neighbouring towns, communicate with locals, and learn more about Libya's culture and history. These weekend escapes were a lifeline for the crew, offering a brief respite from the relentless pressures of the rig and giving Karan a chance to reflect on his experiences and regain his mental fortitude.

Some of the activities they engaged in included visiting markets, tasting Libyan food, and even travelling to some historical sites in Libya. It was comforting to experience the warmth of the Libyan people, and it was fascinating for Karan to discover more about their culture. These weekend adventures were beneficial as they deepened his understanding of the region and its people, making his time in Libya a more meaningful and fulfilling experience.

Karan's lifestyle in the Gulf and the Middle East involved long working hours but at the same time offered several opportunities to explore the cultures. Sometimes, he reflected on the tales from the Iraq-Kuwait war and found numerous parallels with the Libyan postscript. This experience opened his eyes and was quite humbling as he learned about the people and the adversities they encountered.

He became much more aware of the area and its roots, as well as how the past influences the present. The constantly shifting political landscape and the struggles to reconstruct and solidify the market were a testament to his mission. His time in the Gulf/Middle East exposed Karan to the fundamentals of oil and gas companies as key drivers of economic and social development around the world.

Although the war of Iraq against Kuwait was in some ways similar, Karan realized it through the struggles of Libyans. The accounts of the wars and rebuilding helped him to appreciate the richness of the region and the critical role of his company in restoring and bolstering the stability of the sector. The destruction caused by the war and the gradual adaptation process that people went through were clear indications of the vulnerability and endurance of social groups.

One day when, Karan was shaken to his core during a visit to a nearby village, where he encountered a family devastated by the war— refugees in their own country, with no food to eat and mourning the loss of all their male relatives. There were many small children, less than three years old, crying for food, but there was no milk. Seeing this situation, Karan was moved to tears. Any normal human being would start to cry when seeing such a situation. Karan didn't know what he could do for this family, so he asked his friend if they could arrange some food from their mess. It wasn't that easy. They had their own shortage of food supply, but Karan dared and brought food to this family. He wondered how long they would survive with this small amount of food. The family thanked him, but because of the language barrier, Karan could not understand, although he knew that they were praying for him and thanking him. In Karan's mind, he wondered what to do next. This wasn't the case with just one family—it was everywhere, as after the death of Gaddafi, Libya was becoming more violent.

Karan met with other villagers and learned that everything started from a civil war in Tunisia in 2010. It first took place in Sidi Bouzid, a small city in Tunisia, when a 26-year-old street vendor named Mohammed Bouazizi self-immolated in protest of his treatment by local officials. This incident changed the entire picture of the Arab world. In support of Mohammed Bouazizi, protests started everywhere in Tunisia against the current regime. This whole incident led to the ousting of longtime dictator Zine El Abidine Ben Ali. Finally, the president had to leave and flee Tunisia. The demonstrations were caused by high unemployment, food inflation, corruption, a lack of political freedoms (such as freedom of speech), and poor living conditions. The protests constituted the most dramatic wave of social and political unrest in Tunisia in three decades and resulted in scores of deaths and injuries, most of which were the result of actions by police and security forces. This whole fundamentals of oil and gas companies as key drivers of economic and social development around the world.

Although the war of Iraq against Kuwait was in some ways similar, Karan realized it through the struggles of Libyans. The accounts of the wars and rebuilding helped him to appreciate the richness of the region and the critical role of his company in restoring and bolstering the stability of the sector. The destruction caused by the war and the gradual adaptation process that people went through were clear indications of the vulnerability and endurance of social groups.

One day when, Karan was shaken to his core during a visit to a nearby village, where he encountered a family devastated by the war—refugees in their own country, with no food to eat and mourning the loss of all their male relatives. There were many small children, less than three years old, crying for food, but there was no milk. Seeing this situation, Karan was moved to tears. Any normal human being would start to cry when seeing such a situation. Karan didn't know what he could do for this family, so he asked his friend if they could arrange some food from their mess. It wasn't that easy. They had their own shortage of food supply, but Karan dared and brought food to this family. He wondered how long they would survive with this small amount of food. The family thanked him, but because of the language barrier, Karan could not understand, although he knew that they were praying for him and thanking him. In Karan's mind, he wondered what to do next. This wasn't the case with just one family—it was everywhere, as after the death of Gaddafi, Libya was becoming more violent.

Karan met with other villagers and learned that everything started from a civil war in Tunisia in 2010. It first took place in Sidi Bouzid, a small city in Tunisia, when a 26-year-old street vendor named Mohammed Bouazizi self-immolated in protest of his treatment by local officials. This incident changed the entire picture of the Arab world. In support of Mohammed Bouazizi, protests started everywhere in Tunisia against the current regime. This whole incident led to the ousting of longtime dictator Zine El Abidine Ben Ali. Finally, the president had to leave and flee Tunisia. The demonstrations were caused by high unemployment, food inflation, corruption, a lack of political freedoms (such as freedom of speech), and poor living conditions. The protests constituted the most dramatic wave of social and political unrest in Tunisia in three decades and resulted in scores of deaths and injuries, most of which were the result of actions by police and security forces. This whole revolution then spread across the Arab world, with Libya being the second country to experience it.

In Libya, a myriad of rebel factions vied violently for power and control over the country's lucrative oil reserves, plunging the nation into chaos. The situation worsened day by day, and there was conflict over everything—food, water, and basic needs. No house was left untouched in the city. People started living in camps within their own country. Hospitals were running with limited supplies; there were no medicines available, and the worst thing was there was no future, no timeline for when this would get settled. People started drinking dirty water from wherever they could find it. Karan was shocked to see a mother forced to feed dirty water to her 2-year-old child. It was akin to giving poison to her child; this was unbearable for Karan or for anybody to witness. Karan couldn't bear to see any more and wanted to leave as early as possible from there. Karan clearly understood that nothing could be worse than war—it's the end of the human race. This is also the brutal reality of nature.

Crying was everywhere, and wherever you looked, people were struggling for their needs. Weapons had become toys for kids. Is this the world we envisioned? Karan asked himself. It was nothing but the struggle for power, sometimes from outside the country and sometimes inside. For the aspirations of a few, sacrifices were made by many. For the aspirations of men, sacrifices and struggles were endured by women and children. Many young boys aged 12-15 were joining the rebels. All of them wanted to be military heroes and became involved in fighting with some rebel groups.

Western countries were also playing an important role by supplying weapons to local pro-rebellion groups. There was also a cold war between Russia and the USA. There were always opposing sides, and they supported their allied organisations in any country. They were always engaged in proxy wars. Karan's grasp of geopolitics deepened, revealing to him the vast chasm between the narratives spun by global media and the harsh, unfiltered reality on the ground.

In fact, Saddam Hussein was also a victim of the same scenario during the Iraq-Kuwait war. There was no doubt that he was a brutal dictator, and he had no intention of starting a war with Kuwait. This was also motivated by the US, according to what the local people shared with Karan. They further explained that American companies were drilling oil and gas everywhere, and all the major drilling contracts were given to American companies. In return, the Americans promised to support them with weapons and security. After the Iran-Iraq war, Iraq was weakened and had taken out loans of around 14 billion USD from Kuwait, which needed to be repaid. The reason was not to repay the loan; it was that America informed Saddam Hussein that Kuwaitis were stealing Iraqi oil with slant drilling at the Iraq-Kuwait border to increase production. They also lowered the price of oil so that Iraq could not repay its debt. According to Iraq, Kuwait had stolen 2.4 billion barrels of oil from Iraqi oil fields, for which the Iraqi government demanded compensation. Although at the latest OPEC meeting, UAE and Kuwait both agreed to limit their oil production to 1.5 million barrels, Saddam Hussein did not agree, and he invaded Kuwait and later faced severe consequences. All of this was recounted to Karan by local oil workers in Libya. This whole war was nothing more than a fight for black gold. Later, America attacked Iraq under the pretence of finding chemical weapons and seized all the oilfields. Northern Iraq was completely destroyed, and somehow, life continued in the south of Iraq.

There are two worlds: One is created by the press & media and the USA, as most media channels have U.S. influence, and the other is the real world, which is completely different from what the media shows. The fight between the rebels intensified day by day, and more and more new rebel groups started emerging internally.

The situation grew worse—now, fighting started outside of the accommodation for control over the oil block. This was the breaking point. All the crew members were terrified and started hiding in their accommodations. Some thought of escaping, and his family felt kind, but the question was, where would we go? They were all new to this place and had no idea of the local area.

Karan often engaged in deep, sobering conversations with locals and colleagues about the war's history and their personal experiences, which gave him profound insights into the human cost of the conflict. Such conversations provided a lot of information about the human aspect of the war and the samaritanism of people.

People opened up to Karan, and they expressed grievances, accusing America of causing the mayhem. They shared feelings regarding Gaddafi, the former dictator, which ranged from hatred to disdain. While the US depicted him as a dictator, many Libyans felt that he was removed from power because he was against paying for oil in dollars. It was rather typical to hear the story that the U.S. actively engineered his demise in order to seize control over Libyan oil. Through geopolitics, Karan understood power struggles and the role of oil in world conflicts. The flames of Tunisia's civil war quickly spread across the Arab world, igniting uprisings in countries like Libya and Syria leaving a trail of destruction and upheaval. The civil war also broke out in Syria against its long-term dictator, Bashar-Al-Assad. He was supported by Russia & Iran, and the protesters who were the opposition party, the Islamic Organization, were supported by the USA & other Arab countries. In the Middle East, there are two major groups: Arabs and Persians. Arabs are Sunni Muslims and followers of Abu Bakr, while Persians are Shia Muslims followers of Ali. There is a third group, which is very brutal and Wahabi, which believes only in Mohammed and has different beliefs than Shia and Sunni Muslims; they are associated with Al Qaeda and other small Islamic organizations. Now, Karan has a good idea of Arab culture and its workings. He further shared updates about the situation in Syria.

In Syria, the war spread to the northern regions of Raqqa and Idlib; somehow, with the help of Russia and Iran, Al Assad was able to retain a major part of Syria, although he lost the northern part to the Islamic Organization. Later, Turkey also launched a multi-pronged invasion of northern Syria in response to the creation of Rojava while also fighting Islamic State and government forces in the process. Since the March 2020 Idlib ceasefire, the frontline fighting during the conflict has mostly subsided, characterised by regular skirmishes.

Now, Karan has become very knowledgeable about the geopolitical situation. He could feel and understand better, all because the fighting was for black gold and to secure the oilfields. It was either the USA, Western countries, or local rebels—everyone wanted to secure black gold. Thousands of people were killed in every country, hundreds of thousands lost their homes, displaced, and millions were injured and lost their normal lives all for Oil & Gas—that's the reason people call it black gold.

Karan felt pride that he was giving his services in this sector, and at the same time, he was depressed about what was going on around it and in the Oil & Gas sector.

Because of the worsening situation, Karan's company had to shut down operations. But moving to the capital city, Tripoli, and then further to India was not safe at all. Flights were unavailable, and they were limited to bunkhouses, always surrounded by local militias. An evacuation plan was therefore formulated, which entailed a dangerous crossing to the Egyptian border. The company had to part with a huge amount of money and bribe local agents to ensure the safe evacuation of the crew.

Karan, gripped with fear and frustration, had no way of getting in touch with home. Life was characterized by commotion and various dangers; people went about their business and found themselves in a near-war zone situation. When Manisha heard about Karan's condition, he received a call from her insisting on resuming their relationship. However, Karan had changed. Indeed, borne out of his constant encounters with war, this aspect of his character had become numb. He had grown up seeing innocent children being killed, and this had changed him for the worse.

The local agents arranged to evacuate everyone by bargaining with different factions in the conflict and paying almost three hundred thousand American dollars in cash to the factions to free twenty-nine crew members, including Karan.

When the political conflict in Libya intensified, the company had to remove all of its workers from the country. There were multiple problems, from organizing the evacuation with the local authorities to securing the crew of Soyuz. Karan and his co-workers were relocated to Egypt, which was not only physically challenging but also mentally draining.

Getting to the border between Libya and Egypt was truly a nightmare. The trip was arduous and dangerous, with probable signs of aggression and fundamental unpredictability in confined spaces. There were checkpoints and territories of confrontation, making the journey quite a stressful event. It was, however, safe the moment they crossed into Egyptian soil , and there was still a lot of sightseeing to be done.

They were taken to Cairo on chartered planes and then returned to India, which marked an end to a tough phase in Karan's life. There was a personal interest displayed by the company's VP, Gurpreet Singh, who personally oversaw the evacuation effort from the Egyptian border and called on the Indian government for help. The escape to the Egyptian border was tense, but they arrived safely and flew to Cairo before proceeding to Delhi.

Karan's return to Delhi brought an overwhelming sense of relief not just to him but to his entire family, who had anxiously awaited his safe return from the horrors of Libya. The incident that he witnessed in Libya had an effect on him, and to compound the stress, he had some health issues. He had to take a two- to three-month break as he went through some trauma. Karan returned home safely, and he was very happy to be with his family. For a few weeks, Karan just wanted to relax and do nothing. At night, he dreamt of being trapped in the war, and it took a lot of time to recover. Karan spent time with friends and shared the experiences he had faced in Libya. Everyone was very happy that Karan returned home safely, and they were thankful to the company for taking a strong step to evacuate the crew safely. Karan kept in touch with other crew members and checked in on their well-being.

He would forever carry with him the experiences with Manisha, friends, and the rigs he had worked on. They had all educated him on memorable lessons such as never giving up, hard work and being true to oneself. Karan now eagerly awaited the next adventure while feeling thankful for the whole journey he had.

Company operations were completely halted in Libya, and Karan was also thinking of a new job. He had a deep impact on his mind from the events that happened to him in Libya, the life he witnessed there, and what he had heard about the neighbouring countries. This was an unforgettable journey for Karan. He had seen how the greed of humans could reach any level and how it had no limit; in their greed, people become completely blind and do not see what they are doing to their own people.

The feeling of power could make anyone blind and change them into a different person. It brought out a selfish nature in them.

Karan shared many incidents with his family and friends, but many he kept in his mind alone. He had to move on and start something new with his company. The memories of war and his escape from it were ones Karan could never forget, especially the poor condition of the local people.

Karan was still in touch with some of the locals and kept receiving updates on the situation in Libya.

Chapter 05:
Africa Experience & Struggle

At first, Karan was invited for a base job in Gurgaon at the Quad Petroleum office, where his primary responsibilities were doing business development and finding new company opportunities. The company started participating in many new tenders outside of Libya, and Karan was part of the team. Karan was not happy with the job, but he had to continue until he got a new one. Suddenly, in a recent tender for Oil India Limited in Gabon, Karan's company secured the lowest bid and won the contract. The company decided to take its rigs out of Libya and mobilise them to Gabon.

Karan got to know about this opportunity and said loudly, "Again, Africa?" It was a critical decision by the company's management, as taking out a rig from the war zone was a daunting task—it meant evacuating a complete asset, including many heavy pieces of equipment, from a place where the evacuation of people was not possible. The Vice President of the company, Mr. Gurpreet, took this challenge and shared their situation with Oil India Limited. He explained that they hadn't been paid for a long time by their Libyan customer, Waha Oil

Company, and had limited financial reserves. He also shared his experience in Libya and assured Oil India Limited that if they received some advance mobilisation and people were not evacuated fee, they might be able to take out the rig from Libya and place it in Gabon. It was a big bet for Oil India Limited to help a company whose rigs were stuck in a war zone.

Oil India Limited's Country Head of Gabon, Mr. Mishra, was a dynamic person. He said that he would pay the full mobilisation fee in advance to help take out the rig from the war zone. It was a risky decision by Mr. Mishra since Oil India could lose all its money if Karan's company failed to take out the rig from Libya. But as they say, "No risk, no gain." Finally, Mr. Mishra made the full mobilization payment, and Karan's company successfully took out its rigs from Libya and mobilized them to Gabon despite many local challenges in both countries. The local person, Mr. Anand, who helped Karan's company secure this Oil India Limited contract, played a crucial role in the mobilisation of the rig in Gabon.

Finally, the land rig R2 arrived in Gabon, and the next job was to deploy the crew to offload the vessels and set up the rig. Karan was offered to join in Gabon for mast-up and completing the rig mobilization job. Mast-up is a term used to describe the installation of the rig at the site. The task assigned was to move the rig from Gabon Customs port to the site, which in real life required a lot of effort and planning. To accomplish this, the rig was moved to Gabon through half land and river transportation with support from Oil India Limited. Karan was offered a supervisor position at the rig location in Gabon.

Karan was confused about whether to join the rig in Gabon or not. He had a very bad experience in Libya, North Africa, which almost cost him his life. The base job in the company was also not very exciting for him, and he felt like he was in a back-office support role for the crew. Finally, Karan decided to join the rig. As per visa compliance, he had to get the yellow fever vaccination from the hospital. West Africa is home to dangerous mosquitos that cause yellow fever, and once this fever reaches level three, there is no chance of survival for humans. Gabon is a small country situated on the shore of the Atlantic Ocean on the west coast of Africa. The country is politically stable and governed democratically. Mr. Albonso was the President of the Republic of Gabon.

Karan still was not very much ready to join, but he had no options left. In the end, he said yes and started packing his luggage with the crew. His itinerary was prepared to reach Gabon via

Ethiopian Airlines with a six-hour layover in Addis Ababa. Karan travelled with the crew, who were also joining the rig with him for installation and activation at the site. He was joined by some new crew members and some old ones with whom he had worked in Libya. Many old crew members did not dare to return to Africa and join the rig, but Karan wasn't among them. Karan, along with the Toolpusher, Chief Mechanic Mr. Babu, three-floored, and two roustabouts, started their journey from Terminal 3 at Indira Gandhi International Airport. The crew also took some cartons of Indian spices as required by the Oil India officials in Gabon. Knowing this, Karan understood very well it was going to be a big problem for food for him.

Once he decided, Karan had no chance to look back. Ethiopian Airlines to Ethiopia was full of local people. Everyone boarded in a queue and took their respective seats. Karan also sat in his seat with the crew. This time, he didn't have any fantasy about the window seat, only a desire to relax on the plane. It was a six-hour journey from Delhi to Ethiopia. Karan had already asked the travel agent at his office to book a vegetarian meal for him, and the travel agent did the same. Karan was served food first as he had a special vegetarian meal, and he started enjoying some wine half an hour after the plane took off. The flight was long, and Karan decided to sleep.

They reached Ethiopia, and it was crowded like anything. There were generally three types of people: Indians, Chinese, and locals. Karan and his team had a connecting flight to Gabon, so they only had to go through a security check with luggage in transit. At security, there was a big queue, and all the locals, along with foreigners, were standing so close they were touching each other. After standing for a long time, security finally cleared them. There was only one toilet after check-in, and there was a long queue to relieve the long-withheld pressure. Karan understood that life was again not going to be easy in Gabon and to make matters worse, there was no food stall after the security check. It was a six-hour halt, and chaos reigned everywhere.

The screen to display the flight schedule wasn't working properly and wasn't updating either. Every time, you had to ask for your flight schedule and get updates regarding the same from the counter. They learned that their flight was delayed, and many times Karan and his team went downstairs to board the plane, only to return when another flight arrived. This repetition happened multiple times. Maybe in Africa, the rules are very liberal, and people got so frustrated that they started smoking at airports near the runway. There was no information available about flights, neither on screen nor at the counter. It was a really horrible situation at the airport. Perhaps it could be compared with Indian railway stations.

Karan's initial experience in Africa was not going well. Finally , the aircraft arrived , and Karan and his team boarded the plane. Karan arrived in Gabon , cleared immigration , but he and his team's luggage got stuck in customs because of the Indian spices the team was carrying. Karan was already frustrated because it had been a long six-hour flight from Delhi to Ethiopia . They waited six hours at Ethiopia airport with no food , and now six hours from Ethiopia to Gabon had driven him crazy.

He noticed that the customs officials were asking for money. Karan realized that this customs issue could be settled right there with the payment of a bribe. This was a very absurd experience for Karan, witnessing a customs officer asking for money.

After a long journey, they finally arrived at the company guest house, which was near the guest house of Oil India Limited as he had been told, and also near the President's House.

There was already an African cook who had prepared some egg curry, rice, and meat. Karan was left with no option but to eat curry with rice, and for the first time, he also tried the egg. Karan was completely exhausted and asked for his room. He reached and slept without even opening his bag. He woke up late in the evening and decided to join the team to discuss plans for the next day. He inquired from the logistics guy how many rig containers had arrived and what the latest status was on the other containers. He called the local guy, Anand, and asked him to meet in the late evening. Anand was a jolly guy and had been living in Gabon for the last 15 years. He was very well-versed in African culture and was also able to speak French. They checked the latest status of the project, and later, their talk turned personal. Anand asked about Karan's background and was glad to know that he was a Petroleum engineer and had worked offshore before. Later, they both decided to meet in the morning and agreed to leave for the site at 09:00 AM. The drilling site was in Lambarene, 240 KM south of Libreville.

Karan woke up early in the morning, discussed the plan with the team, and left for the site along with Anand. The team was split into two groups and left in two cars. Karan discussed the plan with Anand to have the rest of the containers at the nearest port to meet up with the rig at the site as soon as possible.

Anand told him about the local culture, explaining that people are very lazy here and that weekends are full of non-working hours—even the shops are not open for food and water. All the local people can be found on beaches over weekends. They continued discussing plans for offloading the containers and hiring trailers and cranes to lift and stock the containers at the site. Karan also observed the surroundings outside; the capital was fairly decorated but not as he had expected. People were in the market, buying daily necessities, and there were some showrooms for Nissan cars.

After a while, he realized that many of the cars on the road were either Renault or Nissan. Even the auto showrooms were mostly Nissan and Renault. Upon asking Anand about this, he was told that Gabon was previously a French colony, which is why people speak French, and all the big industries still belong to the French people.

Karan's car began to reach the suburbs of the capital, where he noticed a sudden change—everything turned into a rural area, and he could feel that he had arrived at the core village of Gabon, which was just on the outskirts of the capital. Everywhere, people were selling dry fish dipped in some oil to avoid spoiling it. People could be seen in broken shops, selling street foods, all meat and fish. Karan and his team arrived at the site, which was in the middle of the jungle. Oil India officials had already arrived and were eagerly waiting to meet Karan to discuss plans and start the operations. Karan had already framed the plan in his mind, as he had been well briefed by Anand, and he shared it with the Indian officials. The work began, and red soil could be seen everywhere. Gabon is rich in oil and is the fifth-largest oil-exporting country; they are also rich in minerals such as timber, manganese, and iron.

Karan was offered lunch in one of the containers, which turned into a mess. Karan entered the container and found it so stinky that he came out abruptly. When asked what had happened, the catering guy said that some locals had just finished a French lunch, which had a strong smell. Karan couldn't eat inside the container and asked his team to serve his food outside. He enjoyed his food while sitting near a tree, feeling like he was having a picnic in the African jungle. After lunch, the Oil India officials left for the capital, followed by Karan and his team. On the way back, Karan enjoyed the outside scenery of the sunset and later saw some notice boards mentioning the distance to Paris, London, and Tokyo. Karan was tired, having had a hectic day travelling and visiting the site.

He asked Anand about the nightlife in Gabon, and Anand simply laughed at his question. Karan was a bit nervous seeing this, but Anand replied that Gabon's nightlife is very famous.

He told Karan that he could accompany him to a nearby bar on Lowie Street. He asked Karan to be ready at 9 PM to pick him up from the guest house because the club stays open until late at night. Karan reached the guest house around 7 PM, got freshened up, and was ready before time to explore the nightlife of Gabon.

Anand arrived in his vehicle on time and picked Karan up from the guest house. On the way, he also showed the house of the President of Gabon, which was very close to Karan's guest house. There was limited security, and it was not like the Indian President's house, where you hadto hire to pass through multiple levels of security to meet.

Karan and Anand further moved and reached Lowie Street, which was full of clubs and bars. It looked like daytime during the night, and finally, Anand told him that the best place to visit was the beach club, which was on the shore of the Atlantic Ocean. Karan and Anand went there and ordered whiskey for their drinks. Karan could feel the cold breeze coming from the Atlantic shore and the noise of the high waves. It was high tide time. They both cheered and started gossiping about their personal lives. They discussed how Anand had helped gain the trust of Oil India by giving this contract to Karan's company.

Karan saw the club start filling up with people, with all the ladies—some single and some with their boyfriends and husbands—joining the club. They were ordering drinks and dancing. The music was French, which was new to Karan, but he was enjoying the instrumental music. After some time, live music started, which attracted even more boys, girls, and other ladies.

Anand mentioned a nearby casino if Karan was interested in joining. Karan had last visited a casino when he was with Manisha in Goa. They didn't win, but they didn't lose either. Hearing about the casino reminded Karan of his Goa trip with Manisha, but he quickly returned to the present. After a few drinks, Anand started dancing with the local ladies and invited Karan to join, but Karan felt shy as it was only his second day in the city.

It got late, and both had to leave for the site the next day. On the way back, Anand shared some local dangers with Karan, including the risk of going to a strange local girl's house. He also warned Karan about AIDS, which was very prevalent in the city. Hearing about AIDS made Karan uncomfortable, especially since he was not married yet. Anand dropped Karan off at his company guest house and left for his own home, which was very close by.

The next day was the same, but this time, Karan was scheduled to meet the Oil India Officials at their office. Opting for a walk instead of a vehicle, he strolled the kilometre from the company guest house to their office. Upon arrival, Karan was taken aback to find Mr. Mishra, the country head of Oil India Limited, busy preparing breakfast while his subordinates worked. Seeing a boss cooking for his team while they carried out their tasks surprised Karan. It soon dawned on him that this was a powerful display of leadership, demonstrating Mr Mishra's deep care for his team—a valuable lesson for Karan.

Finally, Mr Mishra came out and asked Karan to have breakfast with him. He asked about his personal life and when he had joined the company. He knew that Karan was one of the crew members who had been stuck in Libya after the Libyan civil war. He asked about his experience in Libya and on offshore rigs. Mr Mishra was posted in Assam in the north-eastern region of India, and he had himself faced such a situation of kidnapping of his colleague by a local mafia in Assam, with a demand for ransom. Generally, oil fields onshore are in very remote areas with limited resources, and such issues often occur in India as well.

After finishing breakfast, he asked Karan to meet in his cabin. His cabin was large and had a scenic view of the Atlantic. He discussed all the mobilisation plans with Karan and asked him to start the operations as soon as possible. From his talk, Mr Mishra sounded like he had great leadership qualities, and he was result-oriented under timelines. For every next step and operation, he asked Karan for the timeline of completion. Finally, the conversation was over, and Karan left to say hi to other colleagues in the office. He sat there with everyone briefly and then left for his Guest House. His team, including Anand, was waiting outside the guest house to leave for the site. Finally, they all left for the site.

After dropping the team at the site for site preparation, Karan and Anand left to meet the port and customs officials to check the status of all the rest of the containers for arrival at the port.

Again, it was Karan's big responsibility to prepare the site and start the drilling operation as soon as possible, as per the timelines discussed with Mr Mishra. Karan asked for hiring more local crew, trailers, and cranes and asked his local procurement manager, who was Gabonese, to place a purchase order for them all. Karan asked the crew to prepare a drilling pad and arrange to transport all the containers to the site, where they would start opening and preparing the equipment. He asked his chief mechanic to check all the hoses and connectors, prepare the drilling pump and other items to check if they were working properly, and service and prepare for drilling.

In the coming days, Karan will meet the Oil India officials, discuss plans, prepare them mutually, and execute them on the ground. His evenings were mostly spent in bars, sometimes with Anand and sometimes with Oil India Officials. Slowly, he started feeling independent and got used to visiting bars with Anand and Oil India Limited employees. He made some local friends and female friends as he frequently visited the beach club. He started learning French, and one fear was always in the corner of his mind—AIDS. He always kept his distance despite having good friendships locally. At night, people became more aggressive, and men's and women's restrooms became shared.

African girls were also very aggressive. They were no less than African men in every way, physically as well. Karan formed some strong friendships with the local girls and started visiting their homes, which Anand warned him about once.

One time, Karan faced a very awful situation. He had gone with one of his friends from the bar to her home, and later, she insisted he take her to bed, which Karan was not ready for because of the fear of AIDS. A wave of fear paralysed Karan, leaving him uncertain of his next move. His lady friend had become very aggressive towards him. In a desperate attempt to escape, Karan bolted for the door, only to be stopped by the cold press of a knife against his stomach. Karan almost lost consciousness seeing the knife in his stomach, and he started begging for his life and asked her to let him go. Somehow, Karan promised that he would visit again, but that today he was not in the right mental condition, and later she allowed him to go. Karan was so happy to be coming out, but it was late at night, and there was no taxi. There were some local boys, and Karan wanted to keep himself safe from them rather than ask for help from them.

Karan walked into the dark street here and there, and after strolling for half an hour in fear, he saw one taxi and waved both his hands. The taxi driver understood that he was a foreigner and approached him. Karan reached his guest house and took a peaceful breath.

After the incident, Karan decided never to enter anyone's home again, whether familiar or not, without careful consideration. This was a very embarrassing incident that Karan could not share with his friends, colleagues, or even with Anand, who had warned him before.

Karan woke up the next day and followed the same meeting schedule with Oil India personnel before leaving for the site with his crew. Karan's work was going well, and it was as per the timelines mutually agreed with Mr Mishra. The company was also very happy with Karan's performance. In a month, all the containers with the drilling equipment loaded reached Gabon. Karan was good at communication, so he swiftly navigated the customs process with the support of Oil India Limited, ensuring all containers were cleared promptly. He further loaded the trailer and sent it to the site.

At the site, the crew had already done all the site preparations. Two cranes of 5 tons and 15 tons were also on standby to offload the drilling equipment onto the site. All went well, and finally, the mast was erected, and a rig was installed on the platform pad for drilling. Some important items were required to be procured locally. Karan had already handed that list of items to Anand for buying, and that was also done. Anand bought all the local stuff and stored it on-site at the warehouse. Oil India Limited officials, including Mr. Mishra, appreciated Karan's management. He was aware of the R2 rig as he had worked on this in Libya, so he knew what items were missing and needed to be procured locally. They installed all the safety measures, and when the drilling bit touched the ground, we called it spudding and celebrated the moment. Karan was a hero in the eyes of Oil India officials as he completed and started the job before the agreed timeline. He also received appreciation from his company and was fully in charge of the land rig.

Karan felt a deep sense of satisfaction as the project progressed smoothly, overcoming minor challenges with ease. Everything was falling into place, just as he had planned.

Karan's health was deteriorating rapidly, leaving him feeling weak and fatigued. His skin darkened under the relentless sun, a sign that the harsh weather of Gabon was taking its toll on him. Gabon's weather is very humid, and six months of the year are the rainy season. He was a vegetarian, so that was also one of the big limitations for him. He was not getting chapati and was entirely dependent on rice and Kubja, a cylindrical long bread. What haunted Karan most in Minda was the constant fear of AIDS, a fear that had been exacerbated by the traumatic incident at his lady friend's house. Karan was not able to get over that event.

He limited his visits to bars and clubs, spent time with Oil India Limited officials, exercised, and walked on Atlantic beaches. The drilling operation had started. He thought about taking some time off from work and asked the company to send another drilling supervisor to relieve him. It took some time, and Karan left for India. While departing from Gabon Port, he noticed a very unnatural thing at immigration: the immigration officer took his passport for stamping and refused to give it back.

Karan was shocked that this was happening, as the immigration officer refused to return his passport, communicating only with a subtle yet unmistakable gesture for a bribe. Karan got upset and shouted, demanding the immediate return of his passport, his voice echoing through the terminal. The immigration officer understood that he was an influential person locally and knew the system, so he politely gave Karan's passport back to him. Karan had the same flight schedule from Gabon to Ethiopia and then from Ethiopia to Delhi. Karan already had an experience at Ethiopia's Addis Ababa Airport, where there were no eatery shops, so while leaving the guest house, he asked his cook to pack some food for him to carry in his cabin bag.

When Karan finally landed in India, a wave of relief washed over him as he set foot on familiar soil. After reaching Delhi, his flight from Delhi to Lucknow was scheduled from another terminal. He reached Lucknow, had a lot of home food, met with old friends, and discussed his life in Africa. Karan shared that there was also a positive image of the local people: they were happy-go-lucky and did not care much about working. For his accommodation, while in Africa, Karan lived in the company's guest house, which was just close to the residence of the president and Oil India company's office. The site was 300 kilometres away in a village, and many considered it difficult to reach.

The holidays were about to end, and Karan had to join the site again. This time, he was half-prepared for many reasons. Life in Africa was not very easy. There was little industry and little local production; hence, it was expensive to survive in the town, and the people communicated in languages that he did not understand.

There were daily challenges. To get to his site, one had to trek deep into the jungles surrounding it; only a few roads led to the site, and these were frequently blocked by the natives who demanded to be paid to clear the road. Karan was a pure vegetarian, which made it difficult for him to survive. Although the crew sometimes cooked Indian food initially, but now they were all busy in their respective jobs. Faced with limited food options and the need for sustenance, Karan reluctantly added eggs to his diet, a small concession in his struggle to maintain his health.

There was much fun in Gabon at night, with many clubs filled to capacity most of the time. The people embraced the notion of carpe diem in that they had to enjoy life to the fullest, and this did not depend on whether it was a weekday or a weekend. However, the traumatic incident involving his lady friend severely dampened his enthusiasm for enjoying the nightlife. After that incident, enjoying clubs was something he could not believe he could do with any local men and women. The relentless humidity and frequent rains severely affected Karan's health, resulting in discomfort and fatigue. People were getting sick with AIDS and other diseases, while security guarantees were assigned to every hotel room.

Despite all this, Karan decided to go on his next trip to Gabon. Nonetheless, Karan identified certain risks and challenges in his work, and he also felt that he was gaining some level of satisfaction from his job. These times in Libya strengthened his knowledge of the oil and gas sector and introduced him to many difficulties he could face later on. Every day on the rig was a good move towards achieving his career goals, and the determination to succeed did not elude Karan.

Karan reached Gabon and met with his team, Mr Mishra, and the Oil India Limited team. Mr Mishra welcomed Karan and invited him over for dinner the day he arrived. Karan accepted. After that, he went to his reliever, the drilling supervisor, and took the job handover. Karan's reliever had high regard for Karan, as he knew that he was coming from offshore and was a petroleum engineer. After the handover, Karan's reliever left for the airport for some time. Later, Karan attended the dinner hosted by Mr Mishra, where he mingled with other Oil India Limited officials, discussing the latest developments. Mr Mishra asked about his holidays, and Karan said they were all good. They further discussed some drilling plans. Mr. Mishra cooked all the food with some help from a local cook. After finishing dinner, Karan left for his guest house and went to his room to sleep.

The next morning, he called Anand and asked him to meet him at the guest house. He told him that they would leave for the site together. Anand was happy to have Karan, as he enjoyed his company. Anand arrived at the guest house and left for the site. Anand was sharing updates with Karan, but Karan's mind was elsewhere. Karan's thoughts were consumed by doubts and frustration, and he seriously considered quitting his job. Anand could feel the difference in Karan; he was not the same

Karan who joined for the first time. They both reached the site, and Karan met with the toolpusher, driller, and company man of Oil India Limited. The number of crew members had been increased, and there were a lot more people than before. Oil India Limited had hired other services from third parties, so crews from other third parties were also present. After meeting with the local team, Karan left for his cabin in a container. Karan was looking outside while the crew was working, and it was raining heavily. Karan did not like the place this time around. Suddenly, he was joined by Anand, who asked what the reason was for his quiet demeanour, if everything was well at home, and if he had any health issues. Karan did not say anything; he said he might be feeling homesick. Later, both went for lunch, worked a few hours, and left for the capital. Karan invited Anand for a drink at a bar.

Karan slept for a couple of hours and then got ready. He asked Anand to pick him up, and both left for the beach club. Karan felt some peace there and shared with Anand that his health was deteriorating; maybe the weather was not suiting him. He also shared that there were lots of funds, but he couldn't access them easily. Anand asked him to relax for a few days, and he would look after the work at the site. Karan shook his head, and both started enjoying music and the beach view.

Karan continued with the same routine while trying to give more time to himself than work, but he felt something was missing. Africa had its own way of enjoying its culture. Karan continued working, but the food problem worsened every day. Despite repeatedly instructing the cooks, Karan couldn't find the flavours he craved, and the persistent problem with food added to his frustration.

The team lacked female members, which Karan felt might be contributing to his dissatisfaction. Perhaps this could also be the reason. While most sectors have a female workforce of 15-20%, the oil and gas industry—and particularly drilling—suffers from a stark gender imbalance, with female representation dropping to under 0.5%. You need to depend on the outside world only. You are surrounded by men. It is a more physical job, and you need to have power in your muscles for lifting hammers, handling pipes, and lifting slips—all are heavy lifting jobs, and quick responses are also needed.

Karan's life was going on in Africa, and days were passing by with new experiences. Karan was always thinking of doing something new. He had operated a land rig job in Libya and was now continuing the same in Gabon, Africa. Overall, Karan was bored with drilling and was looking for something new. There were not many options like mechanical and electrical engineering for him; he could enter other businesses, and almost all the core sectors have electrical and mechanical requirements. For the last several years, Karan had been engaged in drilling operations, and he was looking for something new.

Finally, he decided to go back to India and explore what opportunities were available. He resolved to explore new opportunities in India, with the contingency that if he found nothing suitable, he would return to Gabon. Departing from Gabon was easy, but Mr. Mishra was not happy at all with Karan's decision. He asked him to continue not just professionally but personally as well, as he wanted to grow with the same company. Karan had made his decision, and when he told Anand, he also became angry. Karan knew that his decision would break many hearts, but he was losing his health, was not feeling well in the weather, and, most importantly, was bored with his job and wanted to do something new. Karan's company did not accept his resignation and asked him to think twice about his decision. Upon everyone's request, Karan tried to reconsider, but it did not work any longer.

Finally, Karan asked the company to accept his resignation and to release him as soon as possible.

It was not an easy task for the company to find a reliever for its best, hardworking employee who had shown performance beyond the limit. Karan asked to stay at least 30 days to give the handover and allow the company to find his reliever. Karan had to agree to this without any other option. He also gave hope to Anand that he would rejoin soon, only if he needed some time. In the next 30 days, they had several farewell parties and visited several nearby places. Oil India Limited also celebrated many farewells of Karan; almost every event was a Karan farewell and party. It was necessary as Karan was liked by everyone, and he supported his lower crew financially or whenever required. He fought for the company regarding their increments and even for their holidays.

The last 30 days in Gabon were superb, and everyone enjoyed. Finally, the day arrived when Karan had to leave for India. Everybody was a bit sad as he was losing a loyal friend, a loyal brother, a nice companion, a strong leader, and a party maker.

Karan had undergone a rough ride through life, but all those experiences had made him the person he was. The joys, struggles, achievements, and even losses were all facets that contributed to the narrative of his life. Karan understood that there would be both good and bad times in the future, so he would not be afraid and would be prepared for anything.

Due to his unsavory experiences in Libya and Gabon, the ambitious Karan felt hungrier than ever and resigned from the company to go back to India. Upon getting back to India, Karan also thought of taking some time off to relax and take a break.

The years before had been full of many emotions and twists and turns but also a great deal of learning. Despite his deep yearning for the rig life, he recognised the crucial need for a break. His family and friends welcomed him back home, and he felt the happiness of being with them. For hours, he told his family many fantastic stories of the people he came across and the many challenges he had gone through. These conversations provided solace as he made sense of what happened to him and sought to end the cycle of torment. His time at home helped him to reflect on his past and also get ready for the future. After a while, he relocated to Delhi, where he found himself with only drilling experience and a highly specialized educational background in petroleum engineering. Time was passing by, and he needed to do something for a living. Finally, he decided to take a job as an operations manager in his friend's company.

With Mishra Ji's support, Karan negotiated a contract with Oil India Limited in Assam to set up a 1500hp rig. The project had already been awarded to Karan's African company, but they were unable to execute it due to some financial crunch. In Libya, the problem had worsened, and they were unable to remove their other rig, R1. They lost a significant amount of money and assets. Karan thought he could complete this project by arranging funds from investors or by financing a Chinese land rig from a local Chinese bank because he had a contract in hand. This was taking a long time, as the contract was awarded to Karan's African company, and they were eligible to import the rig into India. This meant the rig should be in the name of Karan's African company, and the investors were not ready for it.

They were also not ready to finance Karan's African company as they had a lot of debt on the books, and their money was tied up in the Libyan war, including one land rig. While this process was ongoing, Karan received a call to work at a new location, which meant new responsibilities. This call was from a port and shipping company for a position Karan had no prior knowledge of, but he was offered the role of offshore project manager, where he would support offshore drilling services at the rig. Although Karan had experience with offshore drilling, supporting offshore services in this capacity was new to him.

Drilling was something Karan had experienced before, but supporting offshore services was something Karan had no idea about. The requirement was in Dubai, and Karan wanted to do something different; that was the reason he left Africa. Karan decided to take on this challenge and was invited to a telephone interview. Karan first called HR to understand his role and was later connected to the MD of the company. Karan's educational background and experience were sufficient to qualify him for any higher position within the Oil & Gas sector.

He got this opportunity, and later, HR asked him to send his passport for a visa and other formalities. Karan understood his core business of drilling and was also aware of what other support services were required for drilling; that's the only reason he got this job. He was a core driller and thus knew what support was required. He also had contacts with rig companies. He could obtain some drilling support services jobs from the drilling company.

This time, he was more connected and better informed due to the lessons learned in Iran, Libya, and Gabon. Karan understood that every opportunity came with its mini-trials, but he was willing to confront them all. It might have been a difficult ride, but all those experiences led him to become the person he is today.

This new role presented Karan with an excellent opportunity to apply his skills in a different context and advance his career within the oil and gas industry. He had never felt so thankful for the experience up to this point and was very much looking forward to where the journey would take him. Karan was fully prepared to embrace new challenges, tackling each rig with confidence rooted in the lessons he had learned along the way.

Chapter 06:
Port & Shipping Life, Iran & Sanctions

He then joined the Mehdi Shipping Company, which dealt with marine and port services, among other activities like trading cargo and vessel management. Even though he was new to the industry, the job's location in Dubai—a city he loved—motivated him to apply. Fueled by excitement for the new prospect, Karan agreed to the change and started to work in Dubai as a Project Manager and Offshore Head. This role marked a significant shift in responsibilities from the rig work he was used to, but Karan's extensive experience equipped him to tackle these new challenges.

This job was more about transporting oil and gas and support services than extracting the oil and gas directly from the rig. The company owned a fleet of vessels and some offshore supply vessels to support offshore drilling activities.

The experience that Karan gained in his new company in Dubai was a breath of fresh air compared to the other companies where he had worked. This new position offered a better working environment, large incentives, and a handsome salary. Additionally, being a department head, he had all decisions related to important matters in his hands. Over time, Karan gained a deeper understanding of the company's core business, which was heavily centred around Iran

Karan's position was in the offshore niche. He built a very robust portfolio for the company. With references from all his past companies, he brought in more business, and his work was done with passion. He loved the position he was in and the management responsibilities that came along with it. Being included in the company's decisions was a drive that motivated him to work harder.

This role was unlike any other Karan had handled in the oil and gas industry, presenting unique challenges and opportunities. Here, Karan was required to base himself at the company's head office, recruit teams for projects, and deploy them while meeting project delivery times.

Karan joined the company and received his cabin with a partial sea view. The room was on the balcony next to his company's office. He was also given an assistant to assist him with his daily tasks, encouraging Karan to work even harder. The assistant's name was Mia. She was Filipina and was deployed to assist Karan by lining up his meetings, preparing schedules, booking tickets, and handling all sorts of office work. Karan was glad to be enjoying the life of a top executive. Karan's new office was on Sheikh Zayed Road opposite the World Trade Center, which was easily accessible via the metro since the nearest metro station was the World Trade Center Metro Station. The office was on the 33rd floor, and his MD had taken the full floor as their office. The company Karan joined employed 200 people, including seamen and support staff. Karan joined a group company, so under the group company, there were many subsidiaries, around 7. Karan had access to all of them as he was the Group Offshore Project Head. Different companies were engaged in different types of business. The company that Karan joined was for Offshore Support Services like the supply of vessels, diving jobs, platform repair, rig moves, troubleshooting offshore, offshore platform or jacket installation, and others, and ship management, which was engaged in managing big vessels like VLCC, Suezmax, Aframax, and Ethylene Carriers. A VLCC is a very large crude carrier capable of carrying 2 million barrels of oil simultaneously.

The transportation of crude oil presents challenges as intriguing as its extraction. It has another level of challenges, and Karan was very glad that he got the opportunity to work in this business. Karan was really happy to work in this company; it was a new learning experience, fun, and support from the team and his base job in Dubai. The office was in a good location, having Dubai vibes. He was given a good team and a personal assistant, Mia, and for the first time, he was reporting to the Managing Director of the company. He had no boss; he was the head of his department and reported to the MD, who was the owner of the company. There was a lot to learn from Karan.

Initially, Karan was given accommodation at the Winchester Hotel in Bur Dubai. Later, he was asked to find an apartment for himself as every company does. While working in Mumbai at Zindal, he was initially given accommodation in a guest house in Andheri West, and later was asked to find accommodation for himself, which he did in Bandra East in Kala Nagar.

Initially, he used to go by cab, and office hours were from 9:30 AM to 5:30 PM, but Karan used to work until 7:30 PM. He had lots of responsibilities, and he had to prove himself in the eyes of the new management. He made some breakthroughs. One was a small project supplying and operating an offshore vessel to support offshore jack-up rigs in loading and offloading drilling equipment. He got this project through one of his friends who was working as a base manager in a rigging company. The offshore rigs had to start a job on a new platform. Hence, they required a lot of equipment and vessels to deliver the supplies from the port to the offshore site location of the rig. The contract was only for one year; it was a small project, but Karan got the breakthrough and justified his one-year salary.

Karan's life in Dubai was cool as he had already lived in the city in the past, so he was aware of all the locations in Dubai. This time, he was permanently based there, so it was a bit different. He found a house for himself in Al Karama in the Pyramid Building; it was a one-bedroom hall and kitchen. Dubai's accommodation costs are notoriously high, ranking among the most expensive worldwide. Karan paid 6,000 AED in Al Karama for a one-bedroom hall and kitchen. Karan chose Al Karama because there were many Indian restaurants nearby, and he could easily find North Indian food.

In Dubai, Indian food is not a problem; in fact, the majority of people in the UAE are Indian, while locals are a minority. Indians make up 35.8% of the UAE's total population, the highest among all nationalities. Hypothetically, if elections were conducted based on population, Indians could potentially have a significant influence. Following our population is the population of our neighbouring country, Pakistan, which is 18% of the total population, and after that, there are Bangladeshis who make up almost 8-9%.

In Dubai and the UAE, you find a mix of cultures, and people live in peace without conflicts. Many are educated, and those who are not try to educate themselves and behave in an educated manner. Dubai is the most cosmopolitan of all the emirates, boasting some of the best nightlife in the world. The other emirates are Abu Dhabi, which is the capital, Sharjah, Ajman, Umm Al-Quwain, Fujairah, and Ras Al Khaimah. Dubai is the most expensive emirate, followed by Abu Dhabi. All the emirates are like Delhi NCR, not bigger than a tier 2 city in India. The Dubai Metro starts with Al Rashidiya and finishes at its last station in Jebel Ali, which is a maximum of an hour's ride on the train. But all the Emirates have good coastlines, and they have big ports and terminals. Abu Dhabi is the capital of the UAE, so all commands come from there. The kings rule the countries, but they are very humble. In fact, locals are very humble; if they get in the lift or anywhere, they themselves greet you with the word "Salam," making you feel a bit embarrassed that you are in their country and they are greeting you first. In fact, you might find the ruler eating in some restaurant with very little security, and they would be so humble that you wouldn't believe they are the ruler or the king. Their culture is awesome, and Karan liked it all.

You won't find cops on the road checking your license and unnecessarily troubling you; in fact, if you commit some crime like drunk driving or something else, they will talk to you respectfully. If you are involved in an accident, it's not like two parties start fighting on the street; instead, they both come out and call the police. The police then check the CCTV to determine whose fault it was, issue them a fine of a few Dirhams, and then it's Khalli Balli, meaning both parties go their way. It's so easy and good that everyone there follows traffic rules: no abrupt cutting, no sudden lane changes, no excessive horn blowing, and it really gives a comfortable and luxurious life to anyone.

Parking is designated, and you have to pay the fee through the mobile app and simply do it. Everyone follows the system, and people believe in following the system, but there is no doubt the fines and traffic fines are hefty, and it certainly affects your pocket, no matter how much you earn. Dubai gives you an opportunity to work, to earn, and to live a luxurious life. They have the Burj Khalifa, the tallest building in the world, and they have Palm Jumeirah, roads under the sea, and ample places to visit. The UAE economy runs on Black Gold (Oil) and Tourism.

One sentence about Dubai is that it is such a place where you could spend a lot of money in one night. There are activities like Kabra, jet skiing, skydiving, yacht parties, desert safaris, and many more. Karan had fun with these things initially, but as his life became busy with work, he was given all the resources, and now it was time to perform in a big way.

Karan's base life in Dubai had started, and he was actually liking it. He not only focused on his offshore responsibilities but also started learning about the management of the main fleet vessels. As a part of business development, his company's MD made a plan to visit Tehran and meet and greet all the customers and meet with some new potential customers as well. This time, Karan's name was also on the list, and he was surprised that in his early career, he had been given an opportunity to learn so many things and was also engaged in the policy and business decision-making of the whole group. Karan was completely overwhelmed and could not believe what was going on. Karan's life was busy, but he was enjoying it. Transportation of oil and gas is a really cool business. It is a bit less hectic than drilling but equally important.

Now Karan became a person who could extract black gold and also had the knowledge of transporting it and providing other support services. Knowing that he was going to Tehran for the first time, he became so excited and started preparing for the same. The MD called his secretary and asked Karan to join him at his office. Karan went into the MD's room after receiving approval from the secretary. The MD explained what types of meetings they were going to have in Tehran and what preparations and documents needed to be prepared as well.

Karan meticulously followed the MD's instructions, preparing the documents and agenda for the Tehran meeting. When they hear about Tehran, people often get scared, thinking it might be a kind of territorial or a core Muslim country, and Karan felt the same. Although slightly apprehensive, Karan was more excited to experience life in Tehran

Tehran is Persian and primarily Shia Muslim. In the past, they shared borders with India before Partition and had done a lot of business together. Iran's relations with India are very old, dating back centuries. Karan read all about this and was excited to see it with his own eyes.

Karan had also heard of the renowned beauty of Persian women, often regarded as some of the most beautiful in the world. Karan also knew that it's an Islamic country, and he needed to be very careful with their rules and culture. After preparing thoroughly and spending many late evenings in the office, Karan prepared his assignments and was ready to fly to Tehran. It was an evening flight with Mahan Airline, and Karan was flying with this airline for the first time. This was an Iranian airline. Karan was handed his tickets; he saw them and put them in his bag before heading home to prepare his luggage. Karan was told that the MD's car driver would pick him up at 7 PM in the evening from his house. The MD's driver arrived promptly at his house and dropped him at Airport Terminal 1. Karan's flight was in business class, although in his previous company, he had also flown business class while going to Africa, so Karan was accustomed to the same.

Although he was a top executive in the Black Gold sector, after leaving Karan at the airport, the driver went to the MD's house to pick him up. The MD was getting late, and Karan could not directly ask him where he was and what time he was coming. Karan was sitting and waiting for the MD. It was almost time for the counter to close when he saw somebody waving a passport. Karan requested the staff at the counter and said his company MD had just arrived at the airport and was now waving his hand from afar. It was business class, so they had to value him.

To Karan's surprise, it wasn't the MD who arrived but his driver, waving the MD's passport. Karan was angry as he was holding up the counter, and the MD did not arrive. The lady at the counter asked if the man was flying. Karan said no, that he would come in the next five minutes. The man was his driver, who brought his passport. The lady was super angry, but again, it was business class. This is how rich men catch their flight; they value their time, and they treat others as if they are granted.

Finally, the MD arrived and said to Karan, "We got late and have to rush now." It wasn't Karan who got late; it was actually the MD who got late. They didn't have to go through immigration as they were carrying a gate pass. Finally, they arrived at the boarding gate, where another lady was waiting for them with angry eyes. They boarded the plane and flew to Tehran. It was a two-and-a-half-hour flight. Sitting next to your super senior can be a challenge because whatever they say, you have to say yes and agree with everything. You can't sleep if you want to. The MD told Karan about his experience until Karan was tired, but he had to listen to everything with both ears and eyes open. He shared how he first came to Iran and how he started doing business with Iran. He also shared that Persian people are very nice and discussed Iran's geopolitical situation in the Middle East.

Karan's mind was also occupied with thoughts of reaching Iran and how the culture would be. The scene inside the aircraft was a bit different from other usual flights. Karan was travelling in business class, sitting next to the MD. Mr. Ahmed, in a light vein, joked with Karan, telling him to wear a bulletproof jacket—otherwise, this was a serious trip. Karan first noticed the cultural differences that set this place apart. The women were all covered up, except for their faces, and even the air hostesses wore this attire. The captain, a tall and healthy Iranian, reflected how beautiful this country is.

The Iranian faces of men always appeared serious, and they looked like they were always at war. But this is somewhat true because of many reasons. Iran is known for its history, especially its Persian history. In the past, they had fought many battles and won them. They have hundreds of years of history of which every Iranian feels proud. They had civil wars in 1978, and after that, they were engaged in war with Iraq. The new regime at that time was not at all pro-America, and they killed many diplomats during the conflict with the US in Tehran. Since then, America has placed Iran on the sanctions list. It's impressive that despite having been sanctioned for the last 30 years, they are still surviving well, and the credit goes to companies like ours who have supported them in their time of need. Karan's company MD, Mr. Ahmed, was also a Shia Muslim, and he had a high level of regard for Iran and his religion, but at the same time, he never forgot that he is a businessman, too.

The flight landed, and the MD told Karan that they have a local team and office there, not under the company name but operating with a different name. He also mentioned that the driver would be arriving and asked Karan to coordinate with him. After immigration, he entered the land of Persia and felt very good. There were men and women around, both of whom were meeting their relatives very gracefully. Karan saw that all the women were covered from head to toe except for their faces; everything else was covered with a burqa. There was no doubt they were beautiful, and the men were also handsome and good-looking. Most of them looked like Europeans but with better skin. The company's MD and Karan met the driver. The driver greeted them with something in the Persian language for a long time, and Karan was surprised that everybody greeted each other by kissing on both cheeks like Europeans do. Later, the MD told him this is the way in Iran to greet each other. Even men greet other men by kissing on both cheeks and reciting some prayer. It was something new for

Karan, but he was happy to see their kind hospitality.

Karan left the Imam Khomeini International Airport and headed to the hotel, which was in Vanak Square, the centre of Tehran. The MD told Karan that it would take almost an hour to reach Tehran, and from there, it would take 15-20 minutes to reach the hotel in the city centre of Tehran. Karan curiously asked why all Persian names sound like Sanskrit. The MD told Karan that Persians have a close relationship with India, which Karan knew before as well, but the MD shared that the Persian language is very old and influenced by Sanskrit from Indian culture, and many things are common in Persian and Indian culture too, which Karan would observe later as well.

Karan was looking outside the car window, unable to believe that he was in Tehran, Iran. He could see flat, plain land and some small mountains. Finally, they reached the hotel, and the hotel's name was Niloo. Karan was surprised to find that this was again a Hindi name, and the MD laughed at this, saying, "You will realise this more later as well." From the name, it sounded like a 3- or 4-star hotel, but the hotel was amazing. The Hotel Niloo was a stunning, Italian-motif place. Even though the hotel was small, it was cosy and elegant. Karan checked in at the hotel as it was almost midnight. Karan's room was grand, and he felt the touch of Persian hospitality. The MD told Karan to be ready at 8 AM the next morning, as they would go for breakfast together and leave for a meeting at 9 AM from the hotel, which was scheduled somewhere with NITC at 10 AM. Karan had already prepared for the meeting, and since he was fully tired, he took a shower and went directly to bed.

That night, Karan struggled to sleep, feeling unsettled in the unfamiliar environment. The next morning, he was on time in the lobby in a suit and tie. He saw beautiful ladies standing at the reception; they greeted him with a good morning, and Karan replied the same. Karan was waiting for the arrival of the MD, but he got a message to go ahead with breakfast as the MD would be late. Karan, without wasting time, rushed for breakfast. He saw that Iranian food is rich in protein vitamins, and there was honey, raw paneer, juices, dry fruits, dates, olives, and potatoes, all sorts of eggs, and finally, he got something vegetarian—fried rice. He finished his breakfast just as the MD arrived downstairs in the lobby. The MD had already requested his breakfast in his suite and finished it in his room. They both then left for the meeting with the same driver who had picked them up at the airport.

Karan was watching outside the window while the MD was on a call with somebody locally, telling them that they were in Tehran. Karan observed that life in Iran was surprisingly peaceful, with people hurrying to their offices. Women actively participated in the workforce, drove cars, and took their children to school. Karan realised that his preconceptions about Iran were far from reality. The culture was more open and progressive than he had imagined. There were no fights, and everyone was speaking so nicely. They reached the NITC office, which is the National Shipping Company of Iran. The National Iranian Tanker Company runs tankers of crude oil globally and delivers crude to their potential customers. Iran is an oil-rich country, the fifth-largest crude oil producer in OPEC (Oil Producing and Exporting Countries), and the third-largest gas producer in the world. Iran has lots of reserves of oil and gas. NITC is the company responsible for transporting and delivering those products to the world. Iran shares a border with 18 countries, including both land and sea borders. It is rich in other minerals as well; they have zinc, copper, gypsum, and Iranian stone, which are world-famous.

The meeting was scheduled to discuss the NITC vessels, which were under our management. This meant that NITC was the owner of those vessels, and we were running them on their behalf. The MD also wanted to discuss having more of their fleet under our company's management. We were taken to a big conference room where the flags of India and Iran were displayed on both sides. The NITC office was luxurious, and the setup was nothing short of a diplomatic delegation. Karan was joined by his company team, along with the local representatives. The meeting table was decorated with fruits and the famous Iranian tea, while the flags of India and Iran echoed a warm welcome. The discussion in the meeting was in Persian, requiring the use of translators to facilitate communication. Karan was more interested in the cultural nuances, such as eating bananas with a knife and fork.

Their large team of 8 members, including their MD, joined the meeting accompanied by a translator from their side. First, the MD of NITC welcomed us, and the translator explained this, which was further counter-greeted by our MD in English, and our translator then translated it into Persian. We discussed the points on the agenda. Both MDs were discussing how we could make the management of vessels more effective, what challenges we faced in operating the vessels, and finally, what we could do together to improve. There was an invoice pending, which the MD asked

Karan to discuss separately with their CFO regarding its status.

Iran is under US and European sanctions, which means it cannot transact any money in United States dollars and Euros. Internationally, it is excluded from SWIFT, so it cannot do any transactions globally. The only option left for them is to depend on cash for their international transactions. However, cash transactions have some limits; you can't do millions of dollars in transactions in cash. To overcome this, Iran has opened some shell companies in different countries and maintains local accounts under the names of locals or different nationalities.

No doubt they have to pay additional costs for this, but they are left with no other option. They have UN sanctions because of allegations of making atomic weapons, which Iran has denied multiple times and invited the UN watchdog to visit their site. Iran claims they are only enriching uranium to make nuclear power plants, not enriching it enough to make an atomic bomb. Everyone has their own problems. Karan discussed the pending invoice with the CFO, and then they left for another meeting. These meetings allowed Karan to understand more of the needs of Iran and his role in his company. Karan knew Iran was quite the oil producer, but with the US sanctions in place, they could not carry out any of their business in dollars or euros.

The next meeting was scheduled with a shipping company, and the MD had to discuss buying some tankers from a South Korean shipbuilding company on their behalf. That meeting was held in their hotel as well. Karan and his MD reached on time and were later joined by three men. Karan was surprised that there was a cop who held a very high position among them. Karan wondered what he was doing there. They asked the MD to buy six tankers from the South Korean shipbuilding company on their behalf. They were ready to pay, but the transaction channel is very long, and again, the business was stuck on the financial transaction and the mode of payment. All Karan learned was that the use of local credit and debit cards was the only form of transaction inside Iran.

Once the meeting finished, Karan asked the MD what the cop was doing there. The MD replied that in all the big corporations, there is one government official to have control.

The meeting continued until the late evening, mainly with ship owners, cargo traders, and some with oil and gas companies.

Late in the evening, Karan and the MD arrived at the hotel, and they both were exhausted, but the MD informed Karan that they also had to go out for dinner and meet somebody. Karan had already finished five meetings, and this was the sixth. Luckily, in every meeting, there had been a good amount of refreshment to keep his energy going.

Karan took off his suit and tie and lay on the bed for some time. He wore a polo t-shirt and jeans with casual shoes he had brought with him. He got ready at 9 o'clock and came down to start chatting with the receptionist, who was about to leave after finishing her shift. There was no doubt she was a beautiful woman, and Karan was trying to capture the local feeling. This time, they were meeting with Jawad, who was an MD friend and a local businessman. In the past, our company had done good business through Jawad. He owns a good restaurant in the north of Iran, which is a posh area with some scenic views of the mountains. Tehran has hilly terrain, and in summer, it is very hot, while in winter, the temperature reaches up to -15 degrees Celsius. They went to his restaurant, and the MD introduced Karan to Jawad. Jawad was glad to know about Karan as he worked offshore and was a petroleum engineer, too. Jawad asked about Karan's African experience and also shared that he owned some businesses in Africa as well.

Karan was also glad to meet Jawad; more than that, he was observing outside and inside the restaurant. He was really struck by how beautiful the Persians were and many families were in the restaurant. There was lots of traffic while they were coming to meet Jawad. In fact, the traffic was heavy all the time. Karan noticed that there was no fear of war or sanctions or any of the challenges they had been facing for the last 30 years. It didn't seem like they were deprived of all European products; they had access to all the European brands and even American products too. Everyone was carrying iPhones. It felt like they were in Europe, not Iran.

There was ample food, people were living luxurious lives, and there was sufficient employment. Karan was puzzled at how, despite the sanctions, the locals were still able to enjoy such amenities

In the end, Karan and the MD reached the hotel late at night, and Karan was left with confusing thoughts and noticed a significant difference between what he had thought and what was happening on the ground.

Karan had another day lined up; he was learning about the company business, their connections, and most importantly, the ways they were conducting business under sanctions. After three days, Karan and the MD returned to the UAE.

The MD's driver was at the airport, and the MD's home was also nearby; actually, he had a villa. The MD asked Karan to take a taxi and go home. It had been a very exhausting trip. The next day was a workday. Karan's weekends were on Friday and Saturday as per UAE policies and Muslim weekend practices, and only recently did they start following international work days. The weekend was good at that time. Additionally, Karan used to go to the office and schedule some other meetings too, while in the evening until late night, he enjoyed the clubs. Soon, there was another trip to Tehran, and it was similar to the last one. By then, Karan had learned the way of doing business in Iran and the way of bypassing sanctions. Now, sanctions meant nothing to him; he was able to source and deliver any items to any part of the world. He had become an expert; he began having his own network of people globally. He developed contacts at ports, with customs officials, and with some influential and elite people.

He supplied offshore supply vessels, platform supply vessels, barges, jack-up barges, and crew boats. He needed to close deals and finalise commercial agreements. He also had the opportunity to work with the largest company in the region, Saudi Aramco. They requested two jack-up accommodation barges, and the rate they offered was phenomenal. The contract was for five years.

In this way, Karan grew the company business in the region. He started travelling to Kuwait and Qatar and meeting with potential clients. Earlier, Karan's company was focused on Iran, but Karan took it to new heights. He started approaching all the major players in the GCC. He went to Bahrain, Qatar, and Oman and secured small and big contracts.

Apart from the offshore and port projects, Karan was also put in charge of overseeing the ongoing activities carried out in the organisation. This involved managing the vessel fleet by ensuring that vessel maintenance and operations were done within the scheduled time. He closely collaborated with the operations team so that the utilisation of resources was maximised to improve productivity. Karan was also involved in building customer and partner relationships to maintain good network relations within the industry. He started making contacts with local Arabs and Sheiks. Although his work could sometimes be very demanding, Karan enjoyed living in Dubai because the place was opulent. It offered a high standard of living, with deluxe accommodations, fine dining, and a happening social life.

Karan attended quite a few networking events and industrial conferences that put him in touch with others in the field. These were not only enjoyable but also proved to be considerably useful business development opportunities.

Once settled into his new role, Karan began to reflect on his professional journey. The experiences he had gathered from his early days on the offshore rigs up to the assignments in Libya, Africa, and Dubai had formed a learning curve in grooming the professional in him. Each of the challenges added to his experiences on the learning graph, and he was thankful for the opportunities that came his way. Karan knew that it was not going to be a bed of roses in the future, but he was willing to take whatever came.

Building relationships between the company and the clients or partners was one of the most important aspects of Karan's job. He had realized that good relations are very important for any business to thrive, so he continued making new connections and maintaining them. As a result, he managed to secure many new contracts and partnerships, helping the company expand beyond its previous boundaries.

Besides making headway in his professional career, Karan also dedicated some time to community activities. He engaged in a couple of charitable projects in Syria that touched on areas related to education and healthcare for refugees and their families. Karan believed that it was imperative to contribute to society in a positive manner, and he had the will to use his resources and influence to stand by the needy.

Over the years, Karan proved himself brilliant in his role. His reputation grew as he received numerous accolades and awards for his contributions to the industry. Karan's journey was not over. He looked toward the future with a sense of confidence and excitement, knowing that he possessed the tools and experience to tackle any adversity that came his way.

As he looked back now, Karan realised that while his hard work and persistence had played a significant role in his journey, much of it was owed to the help of a plethora of people who had supported him and guided him in the right way. He was thankful for his, colleagues, and friends—people who helped him grow and achieve his goals. Karan realised that ahead of him was a new path that needed to be welcomed not just with open arms but with all his heart.

Gradually, Karan started dealing in cargo trading, supplying various types of cargo to Brazil, Iraq, and Lebanon. He handled fuel, crude oil, base oil, bitumen, aircraft fuel JP54, jet fuel A1 and

A2, and D2 with different sulfur content. He had created a large network of sellers and sources and directly dealt with the refineries. His company took end-to-end responsibility for cargo delivery, ensuring all the proper paperwork was in place and financial transactions were completed. Karan established many shell companies to route transactions in a way that appeared legitimate, and he was also a good source for collecting cash from any part of the world via exchanges.

Karan started traveling to Southeast Asian countries to make new connections in China to source and deliver goods to Iran and other Middle Eastern countries with a decent margin. He established the company's new base in Kuala Lumpur, Malaysia, to source items nearby and from China. He secured some good clients and managed their assets, like floating oil production and storage platforms, and further arranged charter hires in the Middle East and Africa.

Karan had worked in Africa before, and that part he was willing to conquer too. Gradually, his strength was increasing both outside the company and inside, which created internal politics. Although Karan was very straightforward, he also started taking things for granted. He began to believe that whatever he was doing was right for the company, but this philosophy doesn't work in a company; you have to work under the policies of the organization. Karan started coming late to work and caught everyone's attention. He was going so late that nobody recognised him. As the company grew, new policies started being implemented by HR. Some were acceptable, and some were unacceptable. Accounts also started their own policies regarding submitting bills for everything, which Karan did not like, and he started having heated discussions with the CFO and all. However, things were tolerated as the MD was fond of Karan and supported him despite some complaints from Accounts. Business was growing through Karan, so the MD was also enjoying this. Yet somehow, in spite of the sanctions in place, Iran managed to sell its crude and acquire the equipment it sorely needed through companies such as Karan's, through a vastly complicated network of shell companies in Europe and the UAE. It was a very delicate operation.

Vessels from Iran could not dock at any port, so there were ship-to-ship cargo transfers on the high seas. Bunkering arrangements were made in Singapore, Sri Lanka, and sometimes in Bangladesh, and a major portion of the crude was sold to China and North Korea at very competitive prices.

These operations were executed through the company owned by Karan, ensuring that all the operations were legitimate. He manipulated all the documents and claimed the origin of the cargo as Iraq or Bahrain, charging around $100-50k per transaction for legitimate paperwork.

Karan's company became very vital in this tangled chain of business, taking care of the ships, changing the source of the cargo, and then switching it back again before getting it to its final destination, which was assured of its safety. His fleet expanded to include ethanol and bitumen tankers. Karan's skills in the business earned him many lucrative rewards. He lived an opulent life in Dubai, socialising with friends in pubs and bars and expanding the company's reach to offshore structures, such as installing jackets and platforms for well drilling.

This is a story of resilience and persistence on his part. After countless challenges and obstacles were thrown his way, he remained committed to his dream. Through focused effort and dogged perseverance, he broke through to success and made a difference that had positive reverberations in the world around him. With determination and a high degree of willingness to take risks, the impossible was made possible.

Even as Karan looked toward the future, he never wavered from his goals and ambitions. He knew the journey was going to be tough, but he definitely had to persist. And thus, with the help of experience, the right skills, and determination, Karan was focused on moving ahead and making a real impact in offshore and port operations.

Karan also held responsibilities related to dealing with ports, supplying equipment to vessels, overseeing the management of crews onboard, managing bunkering operations, and signing charter party agreements. He frequently visited ports and spent long periods on vessels while berthing there, getting to know the crew and their operations for proper management.

The voice against Karan internally was getting stronger as he was holding a major part of the Group's business. These voices against Karan were starting to echo in the MD's ear. Karan also became adamant about many things since he began to realize that the company was working and getting business because of his name. Soon, a project that Karan concluded with an Iranian company worth $30M was transferred to a captain who had just joined the company in India, and the captain was asked to come and join the Dubai office. Karan did not like this behavior of the company. This is how it happens in the corporate world. Karan's dreams and expectations were also growing with the business he was bringing into the company. He started looking for other opportunities and a second source of income.

He became less responsible, and this was clearly visible in his activities. The MD was also watching this, but in the end, he was a businessman. In the meantime, there was news that Karan's vessel was arrested in Yemen and the crew got kidnapped.

Karan had traveled through some of the most turbulent regions and situations imaginable. He was now entering yet another challenging situation in Yemen, after his heady days in Libya. He was now a Project Manager and an Offshore Head, positions that came with their due respect and a much greater level of responsibility. The situation in Yemen turned dangerous, and his company's ship and its crew got embroiled in the middle of a civil war.

Yemen's civil war erupted in September 2014 after a coup against the then-president by the Houthi rebel group. The Houthis claimed there were huge corruption cases by the government and an outbreak of fatal conflict for power. The president fled to the United States, and thereafter, chaos reigned in Yemen, with the forces that remained loyal to the government fighting the Houthis. This conflict soon evolved into a proxy war, with Saudi Arabia supporting the government and

Iran backing the Houthis. Logistics and supply chains became important if either side was to sustain its military in such a hostile environment.

Karan's company undertook the supply of basic necessities such as food, fuel, and rations that either party might need, purely as a business proposition. Things only took a turn for the worse when one of its ships, transporting highly prized LNG, was hijacked at Sana'a sea port by Houthi rebels. The crew onboard was taken prisoner, and the ship was effectively grounded. While the vessel had been insured against war, it did not include coverage for the lives of those on board, so the company found itself in a precarious situation.

The high stakes and lucrative opportunities were irresistible, even as most shipping companies avoided war zones due to the logistical complexities involved. Cargo prices could skyrocket during wartime to sometimes four or five times their normal value, with deals often made with full upfront payments. It was a risky decision, but Karan's company decided to send one of the vessels managed by them to deliver the LNG.

Cash was king in such situations. The detained crew had to face limited rations and growing uncertainty. Having faced a similar crisis in Libya, Karan was put in charge of resolving this situation. He tried to communicate with the captors through the ship's captain, but the language problem and the money demanded by the captors made the job difficult. The only clear message received was the repeated demand for cash.

Realising the situation, Karan contacted his Iranian contacts since they had a hold on the Houthis. After two tense days, Karan discovered that a local rebel group allied with the Houthis had captured the ship and was demanding ransom. The next challenge was to arrange for the required amount of money and its safe delivery in cash. He worked through his network to coordinate with local contacts at currency exchanges and local intermediaries handling the ransom money.

The process was tense and risky. Karan's experience and resourcefulness were being stretched to the limit as he negotiated this intricate and dangerous situation in a war zone. Finally, after intense efforts, he managed to arrange for the ransom to be delivered to the captors and secured the release of the ship and its crew. The vessel safely reached the UAE port, and the crew expressed deep gratitude towards Karan for saving their lives. He felt a deep sense of relief and accomplishment, having gone through such perils himself.

He realised that life is very precious and war is cruel. War is different from a health crisis or an accident, where one faces a sudden fear of death, but in war, one lives with the fear of death day in and day out. Karan had emerged as a hero to his crew and colleagues by displaying great leadership and crisis management skills.

The war in Yemen was another deep learning experience for Karan about the value of life and how cruel war can really be. Experiencing two wars up close—first by being in the midst of one and then by witnessing the impact of another—he now knew everything about the risks and complexities involved in a conflict zone. In a war, trust becomes a rare entity, and one's survival depends on the art of negotiating through a maze of friends turned enemies and enemies appearing to be friends—all of them viewing human life as worthless.

Yemen was spiralling into a genocidal state, with many children dying due to starvation, varied diseases, and malnutrition. The war had rendered people jobless, homeless, and hopeless; it had taken everything except brutal memories. Wars uncover the darkest human nature—greed and power that turn humans into monsters.

Despite all this, Karan continued performing his duties in all capacities and rendered important support and leadership. He was resilient and could navigate through such treacherous situations, and this made him such a great asset to his company.

For Karan, this emphasised how global supply chains are interlinked and how geopolitical conflicts can hit home in everyday operations.

In really tough situations, Karan's leadership qualities indeed came to the fore. He kept his team motivated, focused on the job at hand despite ever-present threats of violence, while keeping his cool and making clever decisions in an uncertain environment.

The Yemen mission established Karan as a confident and resourceful leader. Karan's success in handling the crisis earned him immense respect and admiration from his colleagues and superiors. More importantly, it had instilled in him an even greater realization of the costs of war and the value of peace.

This chapter in Karan's life was one of survival but also an eye-opener to many more lessons that would play a very big role in his future decisions. It was all about preparation, being quick on your feet, and adjusting to situations changing at breakneck speed.

From offshore rigs in Dubai to war-torn ports in Yemen, Karan's journey was filled with experiences that enriched his skills and knowledge. He knew life still had many more challenges to throw at him, but now he felt much more capable of handling them head-on, armed with lessons learned in the past and the resilience that got him through the harshest of times.

Through all his work, Karan never deviated from his principles and kept performing his duty, come what may, to make a difference. His story is imbued with the power of hard work, the spirit of leadership par excellence, and the human spirit that endures amidst adversities.

The Yemen crisis had a lasting effect on Karan. He also became more acutely aware of the volatility of the regions in which his company operated. He also became an empathetic leader who understood the fears and concerns of his crew at a very personal level. This translated into closer ties with his team, who viewed him not only as a manager but also as a protector who had their welfare at heart.

Karan's reputation had grown, and so had his responsibilities. The company relied on him more to head operations in high-risk areas. His success in Yemen was testimony that he could handle the most extreme pressure and still come out on top. Such recognition brought with it the realisation that Karan needed to be on guard at all times; the stakes were higher than ever.

In the months following the Yemen incident, Karan played a very big role in the restructuring of his company to implement better ways of dealing with risk management. He introduced new protocols for how to be better prepared for such situations in the future. This included regular training for the crew in crisis management, more clearly defined lines of communication, and contingency measures planned for various circumstances. Karan's experience in Yemen was turned into a company case study, serving as a blueprint for managing future crises.

All of Karan's proactive measures paid off. Improvements in operational efficiency and reputation strengthened the company's standing within the industry. The clients and partners appreciated the commitment to safety and reliability in the harshest of environments. This increased confidence opened the doors to additional business and growth.

Karan did not let all this success go to his head. The scars of the Yemen crisis were too fresh in his mind to forget how uncertain life could sometimes be and how little there was to be haughty about. He remained hands-on with his colleagues, and mutual respect and encouragement continued to be instilled within the culture of the workforce. Karan became more inclusive as a leader, soliciting views from all levels of the organisation. This change in management style improved morale and led to a raft of innovations and good decisions.

Karan's personal life was also stabilizing. His experiences had been too intense for him to appreciate the mundane things in life. He started finding solace in time spent with his family and friends, relishing moments he had earlier taken for granted. His outlook on life changed, and he was more focused on balancing work and life.

Looking into the future, Karan recognized that further turbulence awaited him. The world of international logistics and offshore operations was a fluid one, and things could get out of hand at any moment due to geopolitical tensions. But he was ready for whatever lay ahead. The lessons from Yemen had hardened him; he had become more resilient and adaptive than before.

Karan's journey was far from over. Each chapter in his life added to his wealth of experience, grooming him into a better leader and a compassionate human being. He could now start traveling again across high seas and turbulent landscapes in his profession, armed with the knowledge that made him realize that no matter what comes his way, he could make a difference.

The Yemen chapter in the larger tapestry of Karan's life was one of definition. It tested his boundaries, challenged his will, and hardened his character. He emerged from the experience with a deeper understanding of the complexities of his work and its impact on other people's lives. His story of overcoming, leadership, and the indomitable human spirit served as a stimulus to others who were battling their own wars in that dynamic world of international logistics and offshore operations.

He resigned and ventured out, but seeking salary plus equity, he entered into an unsuccessful negotiation with the associate of an inviting business in Dubai. An Abu Dhabi-based company then invited him to work for them as their General Manager. Excited for a new challenge, Karan prepared to fly one more time and face what lay ahead in terms of challenges and opportunities.

Chapter 07:
CIA Agent & Reward For Justice

The new job at the Abu Dhabi-based company was a significant leap in the career chart for Karan. He was appointed to the position of General Manager, which carried considerable responsibilities and the promise of further growth. The company specialised in chemical manufacturing for the removal of sludge in pipelines, an area in which Karan had some experience. He looked forward to using his varied experience to make the company a success.

With his new assignment, Karan, through his contacts, took on big projects—from the initial conception down to the implementation and completion of works. It involved dealing with the nitty-gritty, apart from looking at the technical matters and liaising with local Abu Dhabi government officials, local authorities, and international partners. The job was hard, but Karan thrived on the challenge.

The company's head office was based in the great city of Abu Dhabi, the capital of the UAE, which occupied one of the most modern tall buildings and offered a panoramic view of the

Arabian Gulf. Karan's office space was spacious and provided him with a breathtaking view of the sea. Besides being outfitted with large windows, it was also equipped with the latest technology to enable him to keep in touch with his team and oversee operations effectively. He was also lucky to have a good team of professionals to serve his various needs. The company was owned by Steve Foster, a British national who had been living in Abu Dhabi for more than a decade.

Customers from Karan's previous port and shipping company were very impressed with his ability to deliver projects ahead of time and his hard work and wanted to continue to work with Karan. In his previous company, he had been working with some customers to construct a new port facility in Abu Dhabi. When they heard about Karan leaving the company, they tried to contact him, proving that when you work hard, a company might change, but the loyalty of a customer does not.

The customer obtained Karan's new contact information and reached out to him to take on this project and deliver it on time. Karan was not interested for two reasons: first, this was not within the scope of his current company's business, and secondly, this project was previously with his former company, and he had no intention of spoiling his relationship with them. However, he also didn't want to lose a potential customer by saying outright no.

Karan discussed this situation with his company's management and owner, Steve. As the proverb goes, "Whom the gods would destroy, they first make mad." The management decided to give the green light for this project and asked Karan to handle it without any liabilities to the company.

After signing the contract, the company had to deploy a local agent to import chemicals from Abu Dhabi and a team to inject the chemicals. The job was at the B-193 platform in Bassein & Satellite Asset. Mr. Mukherjee was the asset manager, and the Chairman of ONGC also oversaw this project.

The DGM for this project was completely behind schedule. He used to call Karan every day at his office and ask the same thing multiple times. Karan got frustrated as he was not getting full support from the company, but he had no other option since he couldn't return without starting the project. Working with the government came with its own challenges; it required a lot of paperwork and registration. Usually, government companies outsource all the work, so their employees end up chasing the jobs from their vendors and contractors. There were some chemical sacks the company had already stored in India, which were imported by the company's previous agent. Karan suggested to the ONGC officials to use those chemicals along with the new chemicals imported from Abu Dhabi.

Karan's other target was to arrange an injector machine with the designed pressure and output flow. He discussed this with the technical team and tried to arrange it locally, but everything from Abu Dhabi was taking time. Finally, he found the pump in Chennai; he inspected it and had it delivered to Mumbai at the Nhava base under his supervision.

Finally, he had to arrange a service engineer for this job, and Steve managed to make a global deal with Schlumberger to send Schlumberger engineers to all of his operation sites globally. Karan organised their passes and sent them to Platform B-193 via helicopter from the Heli-base. A few years ago, Karan used to go to the offshore rigs when he was with Zindal, and this operation reminded him of his memories of working at Zindal long ago. Now, everything major was arranged, and the injection process was started at the platform. Karan could finally breathe, as ONGC had made his life nothing short of hell.

The initial result was that the chemical was effective, and the sludge was getting dissolved. Earlier, the production from the pipeline was one thousand barrels a day, and by the completion of the injection, it had increased to thirteen thousand barrels per day. There was a direct increase of five thousand barrels per day. This news reached the Chairman's office in Delhi, and everyone congratulated the Chairman on this successful operation. Mr. Moitra, who was in charge of this asset and also the asset manager, also received congratulations and appreciation from the Chairman's office, and he further congratulated Karan and his team for this grand success. Karan's order was extended, and he was asked to import new chemicals as soon as possible to remove sludge from other pipelines.

The company offered him accommodation at the Sea Princess Hotel in Juhu, from where he watched the silent waves incessantly invade the city's shore. Although the project had its share of problems, Karan enjoyed the responsibility of setting up a local team and liaising with his counterpart in Abu Dhabi for the import of chemicals.

Amidst these responsibilities, one fine morning, Karan read in the papers that the USA had imposed a sanction on his ex-company. All the subsidiaries of his ex-company and all the key officers were included in this sanction order. One of the ships that belonged to his old company was detained at Gibraltar port in Spain. The ship was Grace 1, and it was going to Syria with a load of crude. The media made it a huge scandal, but Karan was unconcerned and more than relieved that he had left the company six months ago.

This episode made Karan a witness to the tangled international sanctions game and the high-stakes geopolitical plays world powers like the USA indulged in to make their point. He came across bits of news that the Reward for Justice programme was dishing out millions of dollars for information on cases of sanctions violations. Armed with insider information about the Iranian shipping business, he felt he could make something of it. Although it was a risky endeavour for Karan, it was a big game between countries with their many intelligence agencies.

He took the risk and contacted the Reward for Justice programme. Earlier, he had called the number provided by the programme but had cut the calls. Finally, with curiosity and determination, he held on the line, and it was picked up by a lady who spoke in an American accent, asking how she might help. Karan introduced himself and said that he wanted to share some information about the Iranian shipping network.

The lady was not surprised at all, as if she received such calls daily. She asked Karan for his current location and instructed him to report to the

US Embassy in Delhi with his passport or any local identity proof three days later, at 4 PM. Driven by curiosity and the prospect of easy money, Karan reported to the US Embassy on the agreed day and time. He was then asked to wait for a while at the entry gate.

Later, a man with a muscular build escorted him to a corner of the building rather than inside the main area. Karan was asked to enter a small room, and at this point, his heartbeat started racing as he realized he might have made a big mistake.

Two men were sitting in the room, waiting for Karan. They greeted him and shook hands. Afterwards, they offered him tea or coffee and introduced themselves with names that Karan was confident were not real. They asked what information Karan had about his ex-company and how they used to bypass sanctions. Karan initially gave his introduction and spoke about his experience working in Dubai with the same company. He was hesitant to disclose more, and the men understood that it was the first meeting, and Karan was a bit scared and hesitant. Finally, the man sitting in front of Karan requested another meeting, this time outside the Embassy. He wrote the time and venue for the next meeting on a piece of paper. After this, Karan was handed a small packet, which he did not open immediately, and he quickly left the room. The muscular man was waiting outside and accompanied Karan to exit the Embassy safely.

Karan came out and opened the envelope, which was full of money. Karan was happy, as this was extra money on top of his salary. Karan envisioned the possibility of earning even more and potentially securing US citizenship.

He started preparing the next set of information to be released and again met the CIA agent in Delhi at a Korean restaurant. Karan was very comfortable this time and talked about everything, from bypassing the sanctions to how his company's nexus operated in different parts of the world.

For the next six months, Karan continued these clandestine meetings with CIA agents, always at a different location. Karan started feeling like a CIA agent, befriending the Delhi agent. They usually met for half an hour, and at most for an hour, and every time, the agent would ask Karan to leave first. Of course, more than the money, Karan was fascinated by the experience of working with a CIA agent and learning how the CIA operates globally. Finally, he concluded that everything revolves around money, whether it's war, espionage, or any other activity—it all comes down to money.

Finally, the day came when the CIA agent told him this would be their last meeting. Karan wasn't sure what the reason was and didn't ask, but he also wanted to get out of this situation as soon as possible. The agent also shared some information about how other intelligence agencies operate, mentioning that every embassy is less of an embassy and more of a spy house. Every country needs information and insights into how people think so they can increase their influence in that country. The agent even referenced the famous case of Jamal Khashoggi, who was killed in the Saudi Arabian Embassy in Turkey, Istanbul. Khashoggi was a great critic of the Saudi Arabian government and was particularly disliked by Mohammed bin Salman, the Crown Prince of the Kingdom of Saudi Arabia.

Karan had come to understand the world of international espionage more deeply. He had already faced two wars in Libya and Yemen and had dealt with challenges in Africa, Iran, and sanctions.

This was an unexpected element of mystery that was introduced into his life, but Karan did not lag in his performance with the Abu Dhabi company.

Karan had lived his life facing many dangers and life threats, and he had matured over time. Karan's professional life was always dominated by his personal life. He met many other women but could not settle with anyone. To settle down or to love someone, you need to be stable at some point for some time. That stability never came in Karan's life. He was always dealing with challenges, which kept him busy—many times due to his work and sometimes due to his own ambition. There is no doubt that Karan was very ambitious and wanted to achieve everything he set his mind to in life. To achieve his goals, he was willing to go to any extent, and working with the CIA was one example of this.

The second batch of chemicals from Abu Dhabi had been imported by the newly hired agent and injected into the SL6 pipeline, but the results were not as expected this time. The increase in production was minimal. Karan was eager to return to Dubai to complete his port job, but the company asked him to stay longer to complete this injection job. Once again, Karan was stuck in India, with no local office of this Abu Dhabi company and no big team, and for the last several months, Karan had been staying in a hotel. Memories of Manisha and his old memories of his first base job with his previous company also made him uncomfortable. Karan had very little social life; he was not very active on Facebook, and his last login was when he returned from Africa. His outlook on life had completely changed. The two wars had completely transformed him. He had seen brutality with his own eyes, and he had heard the painful cries of his crew when they were kidnapped in Yemen. He had witnessed the pain of families when their sole breadwinner was kidnapped, uncertain whether he was alive or not. He had seen the longing in a child's eyes, waiting for his father to return, hoping for toys. He had seen the pain of a mother, the pain of a wife, and the hope of a son and daughter. Karan had become a completely different man.

He had seen life under sanctions, the false smiles and the greed of kings, and that to become the number one country, some would go to any lengths. In childhood, he used to study war, and it fascinated him, but now, after witnessing war, he began to hate it. He had come to understand that when a person dies, they do not die alone; with them, their whole family dies—a son dies, a husband dies, a father dies, a brother dies—it is not just one person who dies. Whenever Karan reflects on his life, he thinks he has lived and seen the world. People form their opinions based on what the press and media show, but Karan had actually lived a real war life.

Karan's experience in Africa was also very enlightening for him. He had seen poverty in Africa. He had seen people eating whatever they could find in the jungle and witnessed the spread of various diseases among many people. Karan had a smaller workforce in this company, allowing him to reflect on his past and decide on his future. On the other hand, Karan also lived a luxurious life in Dubai; he stayed in the best hotels and flew everywhere in business class. In Mumbai, he was also staying at the Sea Princess Hotel in Juhu, which has a sea view.

One evening, while dining at a restaurant in Colaba, Mumbai, Karan noticed children playing in oily water, later realising it was contaminated with crude oil. He realised afterwards that the water was full of crude oil. Deeply moved and shaken, he began to introspect deeply on the environmental issues vis-à-vis his industry. However, an oil spill in the sea near Mumbai was one of the milestones that solidified his grudge against the oil and gas sector.

Chapter 08:
Transition to Green Energy

The incident that happened in Colaba was really disturbing for Karan. This experience prompted Karan to reflect on his job, what he was doing, and what he was contributing to society. While making money is important, it should never come at the expense of humanity. He developed an immense desire to engage in clean energy.

Karan felt that his Abu Dhabi company would permanently post him in Mumbai, which he was not interested in. He had to look for another option, and the incident in Colaba made him think about working in clean energy. It was a new journey for Karan, and he wanted to pursue it. He needed a breakthrough, which was not easy. Karan's entire experience was in Black Gold, and his speciality was also in Black Gold. All the contacts and connections he had made were also in Black Gold. So, transitioning to clean energy was not easy, although clean renewable energy had become a growing market attracting many investors. Karan was looking for an opportunity while continuing his job with the Abu Dhabi company. He was exploring the green energy market and considering where he could start.

He remembered that many solar companies had approached him in the past to help set up solar plants in the Middle East, but at that time, it was a niche and small market. Karan had no knowledge of solar plants, but one of his relatives worked in a thermal power plant, and he got the opportunity to visit the plant through them. He gained a very good understanding of the thermal power plant. During his college days, Electrical Engineering was also a subject in his fourth semester, which gave him some basics in Electrical and Power Engineering.

Finally, through his friend Vishal, Karan connected with Mr. Kush, the President of Assor Power. He was based in Dubai and was responsible for procuring the major components of the power plant. Mr. Kush had previously worked at NTPC and now held a very good executive position at Assor. He was the person who had procured $5 billion worth of power equipment, including turbines from China, for installation in Assor Power Plant in India. He also arranged financing for the equipment. Although he was in the position of VP, he was in direct contact with the owner of the company, who frequently sought his advice on many company decisions.

Karan initially had a telephone call with him, introduced himself, and expressed his desire to enter the clean energy sector. Mr. Kush was glad to hear about Karan's experiences in the Libyan war, Africa, and Iran. Mr. Kush also shared his long experience in China. They both agreed to work together and explore future opportunities in a win-win situation.

After some time, Karan received a call from Vishal informing him that Mr. Kush wanted to connect with him regarding some projects. They had certain pain points that Mr. Kush wanted to discuss. Karan called Mr. Kush after receiving his contact details from Vishal and learned that Assor Power had two combined gas cycle power plants in India that were non-operational due to the high commercial gas prices. Because of the high commercial prices, the economics of running the plant were not viable, leading the owner to decide to shut down the plant. One plant had a capacity of 500 MW, and the other had a capacity of 515 MW. Both power plants had offtake agreements in place, supplying power to Assor Steel Plant and another to a state distribution company.

Because both power plants were on standby, the company was losing significant revenue, and the debt on the asset was increasing day by day. The company initially considered selling both plants, but due to a lack of buyers in the market, they were unable to do so. To generate revenue from them, the company asked Mr. Kush to find a solution for these plants. After talking to Karan and recognising his experience and influence in the Middle East, Mr. Kush thought they could shift the power plant to the Middle East, where gas is much cheaper than in India. This way, the plant could be reactivated, and they could earn revenue to repay the banks' debt.

Mr. Kush proposed this idea to the management and the promoters of the Assor Group, and they liked it. They permitted Mr. Kush to proceed. Karan listened silently to Mr. Kush's proposal and said that he would need some time to consider it, as this was a new business for him, and he wasn't sure how he could help. Mr. Kush asked Karan to take his time and get back to him.

Karan thought deeply about what to do, how to do it, and what value he could add. He had no experience with power plants, but he knew the basics. Karan understood that in every sector, there are two key aspects: technical and commercial. One doesn't need to be a technical expert to run a business. For instance, the promoters of Assor may not have had expertise in power plants, but they were successfully running the business.

What is important is having a basic understanding and common sense in using financial numbers. After thinking it over for a few days, Karan contacted Mr. Kush and said that through his contacts and experience in Oil & Gas, he could help in securing cheap commercial gas in the Middle East. Mr. Kush was pleased and offered him the position of Vice President. Karan saw this as a promotion and accepted the offer. However, Karan also inquired if they were open to doing business in Iran, to which Mr. Kush replied that they would manage it. Assor also has a large refinery in Gujarat with a capacity of 9 MTPA, for which they purchase crude from different countries, and Karan was certain that one of these countries was Iran, as they sell their crude at much cheaper rates than the market. Any refining company buying crude from them could make a significant profit on refining it.

The promoters of Assor were already familiar with business in Iran and were well-known in the Iranian system. After receiving the offer letter from Mr. Kush, Karan resigned from the Abu Dhabi company and joined Assor. His initial posting was in Dubai, which Karan had been looking forward to, and he was very happy to return home. He had to contact all the major companies in the Middle East that were selling gas. Generally, these kinds of deals are government-to-government (G2G), but here the buyer was a private company. Additionally, to ensure that this gas and oil could not be used to support terrorism, fuel military vehicles, or for any wrongful purpose, the oil and gas companies conduct a high level of due diligence on the buyer if they are not a government entity.

Karan knew all the procedures for buying crude, as he had done a lot in his previous Dubai company while managing vessels and handling cargo trading activities. He was the person who could secure millions of barrels of oil at the cheapest rates in the market and have it delivered safely to any part of the world. This was Karan's expertise—he knew how to handle challenges and manage the entire process.

Karan initiated the project by gathering key details about the power plant, such as its commissioning date, the duration of its shutdown, and other pertinent information, before presenting it to potential gas suppliers. Karan conducted his own research and then started looking for the countries from which he could secure cheap gas. The options were few: Qatar, Iraq, and Iran, where the plant could be relocated.

Qatar was a relatively new territory for Karan. Although he had worked for some clients there, his network of contacts was not as deeply established as it was in Iran and Iraq. Karan started exploring contacts in all three countries. He visited all three and met with the top officials of the companies. In Qatar, he approached Qatar Gas and Ras Laffan Gas; in Iran, he approached the National Iranian Gas Company; and in Iraq, he approached the Basrah Gas Company.

Karan's experience grew as he dealt with significant opportunities. There were two proposals: one was an investment proposal to set up a combined gas cycle power plant, and the other was to buy gas at a cheaper price. Any country would benefit from such a proposal. First, a combined gas cycle power plant would be installed in their country, enhancing the installed power generation capacity, bringing in investment, and creating local jobs. Secondly, they would have a potential customer for their gas reserves on a long-term basis.

Given the nature of this proposal, every company rolled out the red carpet for Karan and his team, inviting them to invest and shift the power plant to their country. However, they became less interested once they learned that the power plants were old despite the opportunity to sell their gas. No country was keen on investing in second-hand assets, as it was more of a prestige issue. Karan, being a dealmaker, addressed this concern by emphasising that the output is electricity, which doesn't matter whether it comes from an old or a new plant. His company was interested in signing the off-take for power, not necessarily in government incentives. Karan's argument made a lot of sense to them—electricity is electricity, regardless of its source, as long as they adhere to safety and pollution norms. With gas plants, there is minimal pollution, though the age of the turbine remains a concern.

Qatar, being a very wealthy country, was not easy to convince of Karan's company's terms and conditions. Additionally, Qatar Gas's capacity was fully booked for the next three years. This left Karan with two options: Iraq and Iran. He wanted to keep Iran as a last resort, so he tried Iraq first.

Iraq was facing several issues, and Karan was uncertain about bringing such a large asset there. The biggest problem was the stability of the government. There was no guarantee that the government would hold for tomorrow, let alone in the long term. This is a common issue across the Middle East, with exceptions in Saudi Arabia, the UAE, Oman, and Qatar. Karan recalled an instance in Iran where he met someone and made a deal, and the next day, that person was removed from his position. Corruption is widespread, and the worst part is when you pay someone to get work done, there's no guarantee they'll be in that position the next day to complete the job. You need to be very cautious when working in the Middle East. Sometimes, even government guarantees are not enough, as governments can change.

Northern Iraq was completely devastated, and in the last 50 years, Iraq had fought wars with almost every country in the Middle East. They fought with Iran, invaded Kuwait, attacked Israel, and then fought with the USA and its allies. After Saddam Hussein, the situation in Iraq changed completely, with many rebel groups emerging and the northern region bordering Syria, being utterly destroyed. Comparing the situations in Iraq and Iran, Karan found that setting up the plant in Iran was a much better option for three reasons: first, Iran offered cheaper gas than Iraq; second, Iran had more political stability; and third, Iran was the only country in the Middle East with its own army, fully reliant on it. However, the issue of sanctions remained a problem. Karan remembered what happened to his previous company, so he was hesitant to go to Iran. But with no other options, he decided to explore opportunities to shift the plant and secure cheap commercial gas in Iran.

This time, Karan had to be extremely cautious. He knew what had happened to his previous company, Mehdi Offshore—they were sanctioned, hit with secondary sanctions, and labelled as supporting terrorism.

He cleverly found a way to navigate this situation. The USA had given India permission to develop the Chabahar port to access the CIS countries and Afghanistan and undoubtedly to monitor and keep an eye on Pakistan from another angle. Karan thought of taking advantage of this situation. With his expertise in geopolitics, he proposed shifting both plants to Chabahar. This way, there would be no effect from sanctions, and they could still get cheap gas to run the plants.

Karan proposed this idea to the management, and they appreciated his work so far. They quickly gave him permission to move forward with this plan. Karan acted swiftly and instructed his team to schedule a meeting with the director of NIGC. The Assor team was not competent to work in Iran as it was new territory for them, and they had no experience in the region. That's why Karan went ahead and recruited a local team, appointing Mariyeh as the local head of this project. Mariyeh was a Baluch woman residing in Chabahar whom Karan had met through Afshar, his long-time friend in Iran. This was not a difficult task for Karan, as his contacts were deeply rooted in Iran. Mariyeh accepted Karan's offer and began working on the project. During his next visit to Tehran, Karan asked

Mariyeh to arrange a meeting with the chairman of the Chabahar Free Zone. Due to the port's significance, the Iranian government had made Chabahar a special economic zone to attract investment.

Mariyeh was a daring and strong woman who was well-connected in the local region. She scheduled the meeting with the chairman for Karan. Karan asked his team to send the agenda to Mariyeh and to coordinate with her to schedule the itinerary for the Chabahar visit. He also requested Mariyeh to book a good hotel for him, as it would make a good impression on clients. Mariyeh suggested the Persian Esteghlal, a very nice five-star hotel in the north of Iran. Karan agreed and gave permission to book rooms for him and his team. Karan and his team reached Tehran, where they met Mariyeh, who was waiting outside the airport. Karan was already familiar with Tehran. They arrived at the Esteghlal hotel and checked in. Karan asked Mariyeh to prepare the meeting schedule, as he knew the traffic in Tehran was chaotic, and he didn't want to be late for any of the meetings.

Karan entered his room, which had the feel of an old Persian building. The hotel had two wings: the East Wing and the West Wing. The East Wing looked newer, but his room was in the West Wing.

The room was very old, giving off the sense of old Persian culture. Work was on Karan's mind, as this was all his plan, and he had to succeed. He asked his team to get ready after a couple of hours and meet in the lobby to discuss the agenda. In the meantime, Karan took a shower and looked up information about the hotel. He discovered that before the sanctions, this had been a Hilton hotel. He was amazed to learn that Neil Armstrong, the first man to step on the moon, had also stayed in the same hotel, in the West Wing. Karan felt a sense of happiness at sharing a connection with history.

After two hours, Karan came down to the lobby and ordered a Moroccan tea. Mariyeh was sitting there, and they started talking about life, family, how long she had been living in Chabahar, and her educational background. By the time the other team members joined them, they were already deep in conversation. Karan asked them to order something for themselves, as everyone was tired after the long flight. Karan's team had joined from India, while Karan came from Dubai. Karan discussed the schedule of the meeting with the chairman of the Chabahar Free Zone and also discussed the plan for the meeting with the National Iranian Gas Company to negotiate the best price for gas and the infrastructure needed to provide the gas pipeline in Chabahar.

It was late evening now, and everybody was already tired. It was the first visit of Karan's team from India. His Assistant General Manager, Senior Manager, and Technical Head had joined him on this trip. Karan asked for the flight timing to Chabahar and how far the local Mehrabad Airport was from the hotel. Everybody was interested in seeing a bit of Tehran. For Karan, it was like a second home. The hotel's ambience was very nice. There were four restaurants in the hotel—one Turkish, one Persian, one common, and one Thai restaurant. It was quite a big hotel, and there were money exchanges available. This facility was provided because no international debit or credit cards work in Iran. Karan had already informed his team to carry some cash in dollars. He gave Mariyeh $5000 and asked her to exchange it for Iranian Rial, the local currency, at a good rate for local expenses and to keep the money with her. After this, Karan left for his room, followed by the other team members.

Karan also asked Mariyeh to share her number with the other team members in case they needed anything so they could contact her.

Karan had other plans for the evening; he had to meet lots of his old friends as he was visiting Iran after quite a while.

There were guests lined up to meet Karan at his hotel in Esteghlal. Karan went out with some of his old friends to have shisha and relax. Iran is a very open country—shisha and cigarettes are allowed for both men and women, with the exception of alcohol. You could say it is also allowed, but drinking in public is not; it is a punishable offence. Karan had gone to a good restaurant in North Iran, where he saw all the girls having shisha and smoking. They were already drunk from their homes and having fun at the restaurant with their friends. There is no match for Iranian beauty—they are all very beautiful with open minds. Karan left late from the restaurant, and his friend dropped him at the hotel. He was tired, got into his room, and slept. The next day, he had to leave for Chabahar. He had already told Mariyeh to be at the hotel sharp at 9 AM without being late and to hire a local car to drop them at the local domestic airport of Mehrabad. The next morning started with a rush. Karan woke up, had his breakfast with his team including Mariyeh, and left for the airport. Iran's planes are old, and because of sanctions, repairing and spare parts cost twice as much. The Tehran to Chabahar flight is two hours, and finally, they arrived. It was like an airport in the desert, with desert and stone mountains all around. From the airport, they left for the meeting with the chairman of the Chabahar Free Zone. In Chabahar, Karan met with the other local team members he had recruited based on Mariyeh's recommendation to support her. The meeting went very well—they liked Karan's proposal and welcomed him to set up a plant in Chabahar. The Chabahar Free Zone officials also took Karan and his team to visit the site where he could set up the plant.

They mentioned that the Makran Steel Plant was being built near the proposed land for Karan's plant and also that the National Iranian Oil Company was setting up a big refinery in the free zone. This whole tour was conducted by Mr. Asadi, who was the Technical Head of the Free Zone and a good friend of Mariyeh. After visiting the site, Karan set the agenda for the next day and proposed that they sign a memorandum of understanding (MOU) between them. The Chabahar Free Zone chairman agreed to this, and Karan asked his team to prepare a draft of the MOU.

After this, they all left to check into their hotel, which was nearby. The hotel was good by Chabahar's standards. Mariyeh left for her house to see her daughter. She was married and had one child. The next day, Karan signed the MOU with the Chabahar Free Zone and met with the local press to share his plans. The local press covered him well, and it became significant news in Iran that an

Indian company was coming to Iran with a good investment in the power sector. Later that evening, after lunch with the chairman, Karan left for the airport to catch his flight for his next meeting in Tehran with the National Iranian Gas Company.

Karan arrived late at night and returned to his hotel, Parsian Esteghlal, as he liked this hotel but asked Mariyeh to book a room in the East Wing this time. The East Wing rooms were much newer than those in the West Wing, better decorated, and more comfortable too. Karan also had other meetings scheduled with the Deputy Oil Minister at his office in the morning. Karan asked Mariyeh to prepare a good briefing book and to meet him directly at the office. Karan had a good meeting with the deputy power minister, who committed to supporting this project fully. After that, he left for another meeting with the Thermal Power Holding Group to discuss partnership opportunities for this project, as they would need a local partner to assist with local administrative work. The last meeting was with the National Iranian Gas Company, but it was cancelled because Mariyeh did not complete the paperwork. Karan was angry as this was an important meeting that had been cancelled, but being an influential person in Iran, he called Afshar and explained the situation, sharing the gravity of the project and the importance of meeting with the

NIGC director. Afshar called someone very high in IRGC (Iran Revolutionary Guard Corps), which is under sanction and responsible for Iran's internal and external affairs. The head of the IRGC is Imam Khamenei, who is the Supreme Leader of Iran. In no time, Karan received a call from Afshar informing him that a meeting was scheduled and that he, along with his team, could go directly to the director's office and meet him. Seeing this, Mariyeh and her team were impressed that their boss, Karan, was such an influential person in their country.

The meeting with NIGC went well, and they committed to supplying gas for this project at a very good price and also agreed to provide infrastructure up to the plant location. Karan and his team took the night flight and returned to India to share the update with the CEO and Mr. Kush. Everyone was very happy with Karan's performance, as on his first trip, he secured an agreement and lined up all the resources required for this project. The next step was to submit a detailed project report and investment deck from Karan's company.

After this, Karan made many trips to Iran, sometimes with Mr. Kush. He also took the project to an execution level. They froze the gas price with NIGC and secured subsidies from the Chabahar

Free Zone. Karan visited many other parts of Iran, including Zahedan, which is on the border of Iran and Afghanistan.

He also visited some nearby projects to ensure the safe logistics of transporting the power plant from India to Chabahar.

The project was progressing well until the final discussions with the banks. The debt on the two power plant assets had become too high, and before mobilising the whole plant, they had to clear the entire debt. The loan could not be restructured or renegotiated because both assets were being moved to a sanctioned country, and Indian banks are not allowed to conduct business in a sanctioned country, as they would have to show the debt in their books. The project became stuck, and there was uncertainty about the next steps. The promoters also slowed down in this direction. Karan's fast-paced life again came to a halt and became slow. Everything had started with lots of energy but later became sluggish. People in Iran were calling Karan, wanting to know about his next plan.

The company started focusing on new projects, and Mr. Kush was promoted to the position of CTO (Chief Technical Officer). However, it was only Karan who gained nothing after so much hard work. This happened many times to Karan. One important thing was that he gained valuable experience, which holds a lot of value in the market. Karan decided to move on and continue his journey in clean energy, and he started looking for another job. He was tired of switching jobs and now wanted to settle somewhere in Dubai for a long time. He was looking for a desk job; he had travelled extensively in the last decade, and now he wanted peace and a routine life. Karan felt it had become too much for him.

Karan's thinking was changing now. Instead of chasing money, he was more focused on giving something back to society. He wanted to create a green and cleaner world with no war, no pollution, and everything clean and fresh. Karan, on the other hand, never gave up. He continued his pursuit of opportunities in clean energy. Market trends were slowly changing, and the world was becoming very serious about climate change. He was contacted by a US company through mutual contacts that dealt with manufacturing lithium-ion cells. His major interest was in solar, but he was also clear that without batteries, grid stabilisation and 24x7 power supply were not possible. Karan had seen enough phases of his life. He wanted a desk job, and he found this company's culture really cool. It was an American company, and the Chief Executive Officer was a very friendly person. Karan liked the culture of American companies, and he was also willing to move to the USA. He had worked enough in the Middle East, Africa, and Asia, and now it was time for him to move to America. He accepted the offer from the US company, although it was not as big compared to the companies he had worked for before, but Karan was sure he would make it big. He was offered the position of Vice President (Strategic Partnerships). Karan liked the position as it offered company project equity along with other perks.

Karan felt that American companies or MNCs have a much better culture than any other companies, especially Indian ones. They care for and respect their employees. It was time for Karan to enter the White Gold space, for which he did not have much experience, but he was ready to take on the challenge. This job was more about passion than necessity.

Chapter 09
Beginning of White Gold Era

With the promise of setting up a largest lithium ion cells manufacturing plant in the Middle East, Karan was all set to enter in the era of "white gold" lithium. Karan was poised to start a new venture: opening a manufacturing unit in Saudi Arabia. He had his first call with the CEO of the company, Who was a young dynamic person from IIT Delhi, later shifted to the USA for his PHD program under the Nobel Laureate who received his Nobel prize in the discovery of lithium ion batteries.

He was ready to explore opportunities for sales in different regions. Sustainability, through job creation, innovation, and economic growth, is the theme of the new venture.

Going from a rig to clean energy was a journey of resilience and adaptability for Karan. Each experience that he had undergone had very well shaped him and imparted great lessons that were being applied in his new venture. He knew exactly what he wanted: to make a colossal impact in the region of clean energy and add to a world that will truly be green and sustainable.

As Karan went about setting up his new business, he steadfastly believed in the principles that, one after the other, had guided him through his career: integrity, perseverance, and a relentless pursuit of excellence that lay in his backbone. His determination to fight through any odds and to successfully realise his vision stemmed from an inner cauldron of passions for a positive legacy.

Karan joined the new US company and left Assor and this was the first time he was working for an American company. Initially he was based out of Dubai and it was a transition of job for him so he took some holidays and came back to India.

Karan had to learn more about the lithium ion batteries. How they function and most important he sells in the market. Along with spending time in India, Karan started to read about the company and its product. Company had no problem if he had been working from India as till no company was having an office in New York.

Karan was the first Outside employee of the company out of the USA. Karan was also happy that he had no constraint in the location and but he was not taking this a s granted. Of -course had to go back to Dubai and start his mission of setting up the first lithium ion cell manufacturing facility in Saudi Arabia .

Karan was amazed to learn many things about the White Gold sector. There is actually very limited production of lithium-ion cells, mostly in China, and the applications of lithium-ion batteries are vast. Karan had only known about lead-acid batteries before, but after discovering the uses of lithium-ion batteries, he was astonished. He had some idea that lithium-ion batteries are used in mobile phones and laptops, but he had never bothered to explore further as it was not his core sector. In the company's incorporated deck, he saw that lithium-ion batteries are used to make EVs and can be integrated with solar and wind power to supply round-the-clock power. They are also highly required in the telecom industry for powering telecom towers, in military applications for submarines and drones, and in small ships and aircraft, which can also be powered by lithium-ion batteries. This was altogether new knowledge for Karan. Until now, he had believed that everything could only be run by Black Gold (oil), and now this new source of energy could make it possible too. Karan found it very interesting. He had knowledge of the extraction, transportation, storage, and application of Black Gold and its by-products, and now this new thing—lithium-ion batteries—could replace crude oil and have a positive impact on the environment.

Karan never thought that the use of oil could be replaced by any other source of energy, and it wasn't just Karan—millions of people would have thought the same. But change! As we say, change is the law of nature. Whether you like it or not, it has to happen. Karan was also witnessing this big change. He wanted to understand more about this, as it could revolutionise the power source for many industries. He started researching more about it on the internet. He found that the world had already moved in the direction of green energy and had been working on this for the last 3-4 years. Karan was surprised that he was not aware of this at all. He had thought that he was going to bring change, but many companies were already working on it. They had installed many solar and wind plants, and governments were providing huge subsidies for these types of projects.

In fact, they were buying power from solar and wind at premium prices. Karan's curiosity was increasing as he wanted to know more about it. He had been completely immersed in the world of Black Gold, but now this clean power and White Gold were captivating his attention.

He also found that work had begun on using electric vehicles, and one American company, Tesla, was making billions from them. They were the front-runner in the manufacturing of EVs, and people were eager to buy EVs from them. Other automakers like Toyota and Volkswagen were also looking to enter this growing sector. Many companies were setting up solar and wind plants at a good pace.

Karan found this to be a very interesting subject, one that could lead to a significant change in the world. He started working more on this and began discussing the sector within his circle. Everyone in his circle appreciated his decision and agreed that this was the future, encouraging Karan to make it big.

Karan was about to leave for Dubai, UAE. In the meantime, he was in daily communication with his company CEO to discuss strategy. His US company was more focused on technology, research, and development, and they were building the first American Gigafactory in a joint venture with an Australian-based public listed company. This US plant was in Endicott, a four-hour drive from New York

Karan had been given the responsibility to set up the Gigafactory in Saudi Arabia, for which he had already initiated work on the ground. Through his contacts, he found that one of his friends was the board director of Saudi Kayan, one of the largest companies in chemical manufacturing. Chemicals are also required in lithium-ion cells.

Cells essentially generate current through chemical reactions. In lithium-ion cells, one important component is the electrolyte, and other components, like electrodes, are also chemically driven. Karan thought this company could be interesting, so he decided to play some hits and misses. He approached his friend, who appreciated Karan for this type of initiative and introduced him to his colleague, who was the head of one of the subsidiary companies of Saudi Kayan. Karan felt very good; whoever he shared with he had started his career in clean energy, and White Gold was appreciative.

Karan started communicating with his friend and brought his team into the discussion, which went well. After gaining confidence in the company's product and business, they also agreed to sign a memorandum of understanding with Karan's new company. Karan felt good; at least he had achieved the initial breakthrough, but there was still a lot more to do on the ground. This was the initial phase, and this sector was also new—even Karan did not have a deep knowledge of it. Karan thought that before leaving for Dubai, he should also apply for his US visa, and he did so. For his interview, he had to stay in India for some more days. The company had no issue as he was working well and also exploring some Indian companies that were already in renewable power, specifically solar and wind.

Now, things were going well; Karan was learning new things every day about this sector and the new incentives from the government to encourage it. Karan completed his biometric appointment and was excited to go to the US. However, he had heard about the Coronavirus, which had started infecting people in China, with many losing their lives because of it. What he learned in the news was that this virus was very deadly, had taken many lives in China, and the worst thing was that it was communicable. There was no vaccine yet available in the market. Karan was a bit scared of this but was more focused on preparing to go to the US.

The day of Karan's interview came, and he went to the embassy in Delhi. As per his appointment time, he was called in. He saw many people sitting outside, waiting for their turn, with some coming from India's far-off corners. He soon realised there were many who wanted to go to the US and that it was in big demand. Karan had never thought of going to the US. From his first job, he had the opportunity to go abroad to Dubai, and he had been very happy with the local region in the GCC. He liked Dubai and ASEAN countries like Malaysia, China, and Singapore very much. Now that Karan had the opportunity, he was excited. Seeing the long queue, he understood that getting a US visa wouldn't be easy. He was called for the interview, and the counsellor initially asked him about his visit and why he wanted to go. Karan responded confidently, and later, the counsellor asked him which countries he had visited in the past. Karan knew that Iran didn't have good relations with the US, but he had to tell the truth. He named all the countries he had visited in the past and finally mentioned Iran. Upon hearing Iran, the counsellor started looking at him and asked for his other passports, which Karan was carrying too. Karan had already filled up two passports, and this was his third passport. The counsellor saw that Karan had a total of 18 visas from Iran and began inquiring why he used to go to Iran, what relations he had with Iran, with whom he had worked in Iran, whether there was any local office, and what sort of projects he had done in Iran. Karan said that his last visit was for a power plant, but the counsellor misheard it as a nuclear power plant. Karan corrected him, saying it was a thermal power plant. After hearing this, the counsellor started typing on his computer. Karan had never faced visa rejection in his life, so he was pretty sure that he would get his visa approved, but after typing for more than 2-3 minutes, the counsellor replied that his visa had been refused and he gave Karan's passport back along with a piece of paper.

Karan was surprised and angry—why was his visa rejected? Secondly, this type of situation he had never faced before. The visa rejection was very disappointing for Karan. He came back home and started preparing for his Dubai visit.

During this time, he heard that coronavirus had spread all over the world, including the United States. Many people started to be admitted to hospitals and were dying. Further, he learned that it had spread in Europe as well. Since it was a communicable disease, countries started restricting travel for foreigners. Many flights began to be cancelled. Karan was unsure whether he should leave his house, as this virus was very dangerous and was killing millions.

Soon, some coronavirus cases were detected in India as well, and in no time, many cases were detected, and the virus spread all over the country. Many countries started lockdowns, with the first country to implement a lockdown being China. Chaos spread everywhere, and nobody knew what to do. People were forced to stay in their houses; nobody could go outside, and India also implemented a lockdown. Karan and his family were locked in the house. Everywhere, people were losing their lives and havoc spread.

It was a tough time for the world. Hospitals were getting full, the demand for medical equipment began to increase, and people were being given steroids. The World Health Organization declared this a pandemic. In India, the situation got worse; the government suddenly implemented the lockdown, and all the shops and industries were closed. Poor people had no place to go except their villages, which were far from their work locations. All the train and plane tickets were sold out, and life came to a standstill. Poor people were forced to walk to their homes hundreds of kilometres away. They had no choice; many were not paid, so they had no money to buy food. The situation was really horrible. Since this was a communicable disease, every person maintained distance from others, as they had no choice. It was such a communicable disease that if it infected one member of the family, in no time, the whole family would be affected. Every person feared that the other might carry the virus.

The hospital situation was even worse; there were so many patients that there was no place to admit them. The ICU was full, and people were lying outside, waiting for their turn. Death from the coronavirus was very brutal. It affected the lungs, causing a high fever and breathing problems. Soon, the lungs would get choked, and the person would die. Even worse, after the death of a person, there were still chances that the virus could survive in the body. No one was ready to take the body of their relative for cremation. Karan felt like he had nothing left in his life. He had already seen the brutality of war, he had witnessed poverty in Africa, and now this pandemic was the latest challenge. Many people Karan knew lost their lives in this pandemic. Due to breathing problems, the demand for oxygen shot up, and the government asked all oxygen manufacturing companies to increase their output to the maximum level. In fact, many industrial companies that required oxygen for manufacturing their products stopped using oxygen. Life was more important than production. Many companies found a way to manufacture oxygen plants in their factories. The situation was so bad that it cannot be described in words. People lost their loved ones right in front of their eyes. They had ample money in their bank accounts but could not arrange a bed or oxygen despite being willing to pay any amount. No words in the dictionary could describe the pain of losing one's loved ones. It was beyond the limits of anyone's endurance when they saw their loved one dying and could do nothing. They could not approach them, nor could they take their body for cremation.

No one can challenge nature, which is far beyond human power. Every day, millions of lives are lost globally. The situation in the US was worse compared to other nations. Karan was relieved that he had been unable to go to the US because of the visa cancellation. He acknowledged the proverb, "Whatever happens, happens for good."

People have come to understand the importance of nature and the reality that they cannot exploit it indefinitely. It is essential to take care of nature. Karan was reading the news everywhere, and it was a hard time for everyone. During this time, Karan tried to gain as much knowledge as possible about lithium-ion cell manufacturing, including the components used and the kind of equipment required to make the cells. He learned that the supply chain is a very critical part of the process and that having the right chemistry and technology is essential for success.

In his lockdown days, Karan preferred to study and identify potential customers for lithium-ion cells, interacting with them over calls. As the coronavirus cases started to decline and vaccines like Covishield, Pfizer, and others were developed to fight the virus, people slowly began to travel again for urgent work. Karan also travelled to meet some of his clients, including one at Eicher, where a friend from college was working. During his college days, Karan had classmates from the Automotive branch who were now working in higher positions in automotive companies. Karan tried to connect with them, and one of them was at Eicher. The Eicher plant was in Indore, so Karan flew to Indore, wearing a mask and carrying sanitiser, to discuss the electric vehicle opportunity.

Karan had a productive meeting with them, and they asked Karan to send cells for testing, expressing interest in considering his company's batteries for their planned commercial electric trucks. Karan shared this news with his management, and they were excited. Since all international flights were still closed, Karan could not return to Dubai. He decided to chase the opportunity in India while waiting for Dubai to fully reopen. He received a good response and discovered that the Indian government also offered substantial incentives to promote cell manufacturing in India. He was surprised to learn that, 75 years after its independence, India had not yet developed its own cell manufacturing. It became a dream for Karan to set up the first cell manufacturing unit in India. His Saudi project had slowed down due to pandemic-related travel restrictions, and communication with his company office in the USA had also become slow, which weakened the project.

All these scenarios made the project weak, and communication also got slow. By the time Karan made a good base in India, he could not travel overseas; he could travel domestically. With this opportunity, he met with several potential customers and partners looking to get into the Electric vehicle or energy storage business.

As the lockdown partially lifted, with masks still mandatory in public places, Karan moved from Lucknow to Delhi and started meeting potential customers more frequently. His US company provided great support, giving Karan an open hand to work, which made him very happy.

At one EV seminar, Karan met the Managing Director of an electric three-wheeler company. He shared that his company was involved in manufacturing lithium-ion cells and could supply batteries for their three-wheelers. The MD was so happy that he invited Karan to his office in Delhi. Karan went there and gave a compelling presentation about his company, explaining what they do and why their batteries were the best choice for their vehicles. Karan knew that the most critical component of an electric vehicle is the battery, similar to how an internal combustion engine powers a conventional vehicle. In an electric vehicle, the battery is everything, and for a good battery, you need good cells. Karan's company specialised in manufacturing high-quality lithium-ion cells, and he successfully convinced the customer to secure the largest battery supply contract in India's EV sector, worth 165 million USD. This was big news, and it was covered extensively in the media. Karan's picture signing the contract was everywhere, and he felt incredibly proud of this achievement. He also shared the news with his family, who congratulated him on his success.

The Indian government was providing significant subsidies to promote clean and green energy, as well as cell manufacturing. Karan discovered that the Government of India had set up an "Invest India" program to help foreign companies invest in India. Karan contacted Invest India and found that someone from his college, who had pursued an MBA there, was working in the program. Karan reached out to him, and he connected Karan with the relevant person overseeing investments in the electric vehicle and battery space. Karan told him about his company, an American firm focused on cell manufacturing, and their desire to set up a manufacturing unit in India. Everyone welcomed the investment, as the lockdown had just ended, and they requested a virtual call. Karan agreed and gave his presentation, stating that they wanted to invest in lithium-ion cell manufacturing.

The long lockdown had a significant impact on the country's economy. Factories, shops, and services were closed for almost a year, which severely affected the economy. The government was under pressure to revive the economy. The Department of Promotion and Internal Trade (DPIIT), a government arm responsible for promoting industries and attracting investments in India, decided to organise a program inviting all industry stakeholders, with responsibility given to the Invest India team. Karan's name was already submitted to Invest India for his plan to invest in setting up a lithium-ion cell manufacturing unit.

The government was planning to introduce Production Linked Incentives (PLI) to boost domestic production and sought opinions from stakeholders across different sectors. To execute this, DPIIT organised a webinar through Invest India involving stakeholders and the Hon'ble Prime Minister of India. When the Prime Minister is involved, a lot of preparation is required. This time, incentives were also offered in the lithium-ion battery sector.

Invest India made a list of stakeholders from various sectors, and Karan's name was at the top of the list. Seeing this, Karan was on cloud nine, as he had been invited to interact with the Hon'ble

Prime Minister of India. There were big names on the list, including the CEO of Panasonic, the Steel King, Mr. Zindal, Mr. Parimal, and many others.

Karan started preparing for the event, ensuring all his points were well-organised to discuss with the moderators. He was super excited, as he had never been part of a webinar like this, especially one happening in his own country, where he would be proud to interact with the Prime Minister of India.

The webinar was conducted successfully, and the Prime Minister gave a 20-minute speech encouraging companies to invest in India. He assured all the necessary support from the government and shared information about the single-window clearance for all work. There was an interaction between the stakeholders, during which Karan shared details about himself and his company. Karan was so happy that he was now doing something meaningful for society.

Following this, Karan was approached by several states, including Rajasthan, Tamil Nadu, and Andhra Pradesh, inviting him to invest in their state. Karan ultimately found that Karnataka was offering the best subsidies and had a conducive business ecosystem and talent pool. Karan submitted his investment proposal of 4000 crore INR in the state and set up a 5 GWh facility in Karnataka. Later, Karan was invited to sign the

MoU and meet with the Chief Minister of Karnataka. It was a memorable journey for Karan. There was a press release, and the press asked many questions about his investment plans, which Karan answered well. Karan had become a known personality in the EV business.

As per the government's plan, they were launching the Production Linked Incentives (PLI), and Niti Aayog was given the task of drafting the policy. The CEO of Niti Aayog, a dynamic and punctual IAS officer, took responsibility and deployed a dedicated team. He started gathering inputs from government banks, private banks, industry stakeholders, and the Ministry of Finance to assess the total funds available for the PLI. Many private agencies and consultants were engaged in drafting the policy. Finally, a raw draft was made public, and 13 PLIs were sanctioned. Once the draft was out, a meeting was called by the Niti Aayog CEO to discuss each PLI in each sector. There were PLIs for batteries, solar and wind power, textiles, automotive, and more.

Karan was also invited to discuss his inputs in Battery PLI. After discussing internally with the management Karan suggested that R&D should also be incentivised in the draft proposal. He worked further more deeply with Niti Aayog to finalize the draft.

At Least PLI launched, but some eligibility criteria were very stringent. Karan's company was not big and hence did not meet the net worth criteria. Further, they decided to collaborate with a local partner. It was a huge responsibility for Karan to find partners and collaborate with them to participate in this PLI in a limited time. Karan somehow did and participated with a Kolkata-based company, but unfortunately, they did not come out as winners. Almost nine companies participated, and only four companies won the PLI. Karan's company was in the eighth position. It was very embarrassing and frustrating to lose the PLI. Karan worked day and night but could not get through the PLI, and everyone was surprised. Everyone was hoping Karan's company would win the PLI, but Destiny had written something different.

He took some time off after a heavy schedule and finally came back to work. He did not lose hope of setting up the first lithium-ion cell manufacturing plant in India and decided to go without PLI and without government incentives. He started looking for companies to make JVs, and after this Government PLI in Battery, many companies got interested in setting up cell manufacturing in India. It was not very difficult for Karan to find a joint venture company. After meeting with many companies, they found one with whom Karan's company's terms and conditions aligned. Many companies were still not bullish on the battery market, and many were not ready to invest.

In the meantime, Karan received an invitation to nominate his company for the Economic Times energy award. Karan was known in the industry, so many journalists and PR agencies started recognising him. He convinced his company to nominate itself for this Economic Times energy award under the best research and development company, as this was the strength of his company.

Finally, the date came for the announcement of the result, and Karan was surprised to learn that they had won the award. Karan was very excited, and he received the Best Research and Development Organization Economic Times Energy Award. His company and all the team members were also very happy, which certainly increased everyone's confidence.

Now it was time to prove it on the ground as well. Karan started working harder to get the joint venture done. His company was willing to put in the money, but they did not want to take on all the risk alone. To de-risk the project, it is always good to go with one or two partners for big projects. Cell manufacturing is a capital-intensive project that requires a lot of capital to set up a Gigafactory.

After six months of hard work, Karan concluded a JV with one of the top four auto component makers. This company had a strong presence in the automotive sector and operated 29 factories making a wide range of automotive products. This company had been working in the Indian market for the last 50 years, so it completely understood the Indian market. Karan found this company to be the right one and formed a JV. As per the JV, they had to set up a 1 GWH plant in the next two years. Karan signed the JV agreement with the automotive company after many rounds of legal document exchanges.

It was very much visible that they would have the first factory on the ground in the next two years. Karan made a team and deployed them to finalize the technical, design, and engineering parameters of the Gigafactory. Once the visibility of the factory was confirmed, the next task was to secure long-term contracts for the project.

The new JV company was incorporated, and Karan was also offered a position on the board of directors in the new JV company. It was again a new start for Karan's learning. For the first time, he became a board member, and he was so happy. His family was proud of him. He started his career as a graduate engineer trainee, and now he is on the board of directors. He never relaxed and kept remembering his goal of setting up the first Gigafactory in India.

The story of Karan was far from over. He knew that, from this point on, his journey would be full of new challenges and opportunities. But now he was ready, equipped with all the learnings from past experiences. His journey from the world of oil and gas to clean energy was about personal and professional transformation, a change that aligned with the new global trend towards sustainability.

Karan's next task was to secure the off-take contract for the project. He already had one to supply a three-wheeler company, but for energy storage, he still needed to find one.

Karan started working on this, and once the government floated the PLI, they also had to ensure that there was somebody to buy the product. The government arm, Solar Energy Corporation of India, floated a tender for 1 GWH and invited bids. Karan was known in the industry, so every day there were many people who wanted to meet him, and he was busy meeting new companies and encouraging them to get into the EV business. Karan met with one big conglomerate that was in steel, power, renewables, and paints. They were also looking for a company that could help them win this type of tender. They met with Karan, and Karan supported them in bidding for this tender and finally winning it. To gain confidence in Karan's company, they visited his company in the USA and also his factory in Endicott.

Now Karan had a contract in hand for 1 GWH, the world's largest standalone contract. Karan received the Letter of Award from this company to supply 1 GWH of batteries. The contract value was 170M USD, and it was another very big contract for the company. Now Karan had 3000 crore Indian rupees in his basket, and he had concluded his JV to set up the plant. He had everything in place to go ahead with setting up the first lithium-ion cell Gigafactory in India. He started focusing on the supply chain part to produce the components locally so that he could lower the cost of the product and win more contracts. He was in touch with other two-wheeler and three-wheeler companies who were ready to give contracts, but Karan wanted to conclude these first two and then move on.

As a reward, the company promoted him from Vice President (Strategic Partnerships) to President (Strategic Partnerships) and also gave him a significant salary increment. Karan was truly happy with this, knowing that he was moving in the right direction of success.

Karan already had enough on his plate, and now it was time for him to focus on execution rather than bringing more to the table.

Operations started from many ends. The steel company started asking for documents and certifications, and the JV companies also engaged in setting up the plant. Now, Karan has come into operation mode as he has to make both his ventures a big success. Initially, all went well, but as we say, life is not so easy, especially for Karan.

He started getting hiccups in operations. His Indian JV became slow, and the management team was replaced to handle the cell manufacturing JV project in India. A new team from the USA started following the project. The team could not conclude anything for many reasons: first, they had no experience working in India; second, they were not on the ground. Thirdly, according to Karan, they were less competent for this job. Despite Karan's many warnings, management did not listen to him, and the same team kept working with the Indian JV partner. Karan was also kept outside of that project despite being a director on the board; he only attended the board meetings while the US team handled the operations. Months and months went by, and nothing happened on the ground. In fact, in the next six months, they couldn't even secure land for the factory.

Karan again warned them that the Indian partner was doing nothing, but nobody listened to him. This was very frustrating for Karan; with so much hard work, he had concluded his JV, and now it looked like it was going to collapse. The same situation happened when Karan was handling the combined gas cycle power plant. But there was a certain reason—the fault was from the bank's side as they were not agreeing to finance. There was a genuine reason, but Karan's management was not supporting him. He was not copied on many emails, and Karan also lost hope. He was handling only the steel company project of 1 GWH, but even in that, hiccups started arising as Karan's USA company plant was not ready for production, and no manuals and certifications were in place. It was not his fault that he was in India and was unaware of these things. Whatever the team and management told him, he used to believe. They conveyed to Karan that production had started at the US facility one year before getting a contract from the US company.

After that, he was surprised to learn that no production had started, no certification had been completed, and no prototype had been ready from the main line. This was so frustrating for Karan, but he had no option but to handle the situation. Karan tried his best, but it was not in his control after a certain point.

The Karan JV company project also came to a halt; nothing was happening there. One year passed, and the JV company still couldn't secure the land. All Karan could do was wait and watch.

Other companies that started after Karan in white gold were doing very well. They were expanding their businesses and raising funds. Karan's image in the market was not as it was before. It happens when you don't deliver in the market. It doesn't matter if it's your fault or not.

Finally, this Steel company also withdrew the LOi from Karan's company, and because of non-production, Karan could not execute the first contract he signed with the electric three-wheeler company.

Karan also got tired and was ready to flow with the time for a while. His personal life was also completely ruined; he got divorced from his recent marriage, and not much was left to motivate him.

Karan believes in never giving up. He is exploring ways to grow his company's business. He immersed himself in research by attending conferences and seminars, deepening his knowledge and awareness of the rapid pace of development. It wasn't just about changing his industry focus; it was about understanding the nuances of energy production, storage, and distribution in a sustainable manner.

To Karan, moving from the mad world of oil and gas to the highly prospective domain of clean energy was not just a career move but a serious transformation in purpose and vision. Karan's background in petroleum engineering provided the necessary broad knowledge base, but there were many new challenges that required a fresh mindset. He encouraged the larger movement toward an ecologically friendly planet. This was a story that testified to the power of resilience, innovation, and the courage to pursue one's passion despite enormous odds. As he kept on building his legacy, Karan remained well-rooted, always remembering lessons from his past and the importance of making a positive impact on Earth. The path Karan walked, from oil and gas to clean energy, is a story of persistence, adaptability, and vision. If it was filled with so many challenges and run-ins, then his commitment and vision for a positive change were what kept him going. His was a story full of potential change and a reminder of following one's passion at any cost.

Karan's never-give-up mentality helped him to explore other options. He knew one of his friends working in a port, and he thought, "What if we could change all the ports into green ports?" He had worked in ports before, so he knew this dirty business. Whenever you go to ports, you find racks, grease, lube, and generally, all vessels, big and small, discharge these dirty, wet items into the seawater despite the zero discharge policy in place.

Karan took the initiative to see if they could convert these ports into green ports, and all the port equipment should start running on solar plus battery power, and small vessels could also be powered by batteries. They could install charging stations inside the port to charge the batteries. Although not revolutionary, like the advent of electric vehicles, this idea held immense potential. Electric vehicles were also invented after the discovery of the induction motor, but this idea could not work out because of the discovery of crude oil and IC engines. At that time, people were less bothered about climate change. The same was true with Green Ports—the idea was there but could not be implemented because of several reasons: high battery costs, conventional technologies, and more.

Karan believed in his idea. He called his friend who was in Dubai. Karan's friend's business was in the cutting and installation of port container cranes. He was well aware of port jibs, and the same was true for Karan. He discussed this idea with his friend and asked him to meet Karan once he came to India. Karan's friend's company office was in Mumbai too. He reached there after some time, and Karan also flew to Mumbai from Delhi to meet him. Karan discussed this idea of converting all ports into green ports and running small vessels, cranes, forklifts—everything on battery power. In fact, all port vehicles should also be electric. They liked the idea, and Karan also told the US company management about it, and they appreciated it, too. Karan started working on this and signed an agreement with his friend's company. They jointly started meeting with the port operators and began proposing his idea of green ports. With 80% of global logistics relying on sea routes, it became a moral imperative to preserve the cleanliness and natural state of our ports and oceans.

The port operator's company also agreed on the same, and in the beginning, they thought of doing some trials to see how effective this idea was. They started by running the crane on battery power only. Karan worked hard on this, as his company's production was not ready, so he imported batteries from China and executed this pilot project. He found it really worked, and DG sets could be replaced with batteries. The 12-ton, 40-ft container could be lifted with the batteries, and the full container weighed around 40 tons. For the same, they needed more batteries, and it also ran successfully. Karan and his friend's company are working on a Green Port project.

Many of his friends and relatives knew about Karan's struggle from Black Gold to White Gold, as did the media. He had friends in almost every industry since he had such a long career and worked and provided his services in four major sectors, all directly related to energy extraction, energy generation, energy transportation, and energy storage. Reflecting on his journey, Karan took pride in having fulfilled his childhood dream of contributing to the energy sector, though he knew his mission was far from complete

One day, he received an email from Economic Times Energy Middle East that he had been invited to nominate himself for an individual category award. He had no idea under what category he should participate, but he knew that throughout his life, he had contributed to energy, so he nominated himself for the Future Energy Leader award.

He had no idea if he could even win this. He had to attach his bio, where he mentioned his struggles on offshore jack-up rigs, his struggle during the Libyan war and in Africa and Iran, and further his challenges in clean energy with gas cycle power plants, and when he entered the white gold space of lithium. He highlighted the challenges he faced. He titled his bio "A Journey from Black Gold to White Gold."

After a month, he got a call from Economic Times Energy Middle East that he had been shortlisted on the final list of nominees. Now that Karan was settled in India, living in Delhi, he thought to make a visit—at least if he didn't win, he could meet his old friends in Dubai. He went to the event, which was held at the Pullman Hotel, Business Bay, Downtown Dubai. He did not have much hope. He met some of his friends and industry contacts. The award distribution started, and the category of the Future Energy Leader award was about to be announced. Karan's heartbeat began to increase, but he remained quiet. To support Karan, one of his old friends from Dubai, who was in the business of ports and shipping, also joined him. The jury announced Karan's name as the winner of the Future Energy Leader award. Karan was completely lost; he woke up from his seat and went to the stage to collect his award. He was so happy that tears could be seen in his eyes while collecting the award. No doubt, he had done a lot in the energy sector, and he truly deserved it. It wasn't just for what he did for the industry but also for the new initiatives he had taken in the green and clean energy field.

From there, Karan began to innovate constantly for the good of humanity over the next few years—from clean energy to radically changing how his life and the world around him were organised. In his actions, Karan showed that it was within one's means to lead a successful business career while supporting a sustainable and just future.

Another market challenge came from the fluctuations happening in the market. The demand for lithium-ion batteries was growing, but so was the competition. Karan had to make sure that his company stayed competitive on price, quality, and innovation. That meant he had to balance cost management and investments in research and development very carefully.

Another crucial aspect was the aspect of technological development. The clean energy industry was moving very fast, and the desire to stay well in front necessitated continued re-investment in technology. His firm thus invested heavily in research and development, mainly on new materials, updating manufacturing technologies, and cutting-edge management systems for their batteries.

His company succeeded and prevailed because of the leadership, vision, and commitment to sustainability that Karan instilled within the company. He attracted and drove the best talent that could be found, setting the bar high and building with a passion equal to his for clean energy. Together, they pushed the boundaries of possibility into innovation and set new benchmarks for the industry.

The price and supply challenge was getting deeper and deeper. The market started flooding with Chinese batteries at low prices. Karan's only manufacturing unit was in the USA, and the cost of the product was very high. Labour is expensive in America, and so are skilled workers.

Karan had to find some way to compete with the Chinese battery products. The Chinese had advanced their technology to the next level, and their capacity was also very high, giving them good negotiating power with vendors, which Karan's US company couldn't achieve due to its much lower capacity.

Chinese companies have also acquired many mines in South America for Lithium and in Australia and are keeping control over the supply chain. This was a major setback for the Karan company. Firstly, Karan company's capacity was very low, and secondly, there was no other gigafactory so that raw material could not be easily found in America. It was not only Karan's company; any company engaged in the manufacturing of lithium-ion cells was struggling. Countries have increased the import tariff to invite investors and to set up gigafactories in their own country to be independent of Chinese batteries. But even with tariffs, Chinese batteries were cheaper than American batteries. The problem is not just capacity and raw material; advancement of technology is also a big factor. China has advanced a lot in terms of technology. It's not like the old Chinese product with no guarantee. They have improved themselves in every way, quality-wise and price-wise both. Karan is still with his US company and working on the white gold. With low revenue and high capital debt, Karan's company felt the requirement of capital. In the following months, from raising funds to obtaining clearance from various certification bodies, Karan faced several such uphill tasks. But then, he dug deep into reservoirs of determination and the network that stood by him in making it through. He and his team set up the manufacturing unit and began manufacturing lithium-ion cells on their production lines with the first batch, hence embarking on a new journey in his career in the USA.

Then again, they faced the challenge of selling in the market as the market price had totally crashed. In the last year, the prices of lithium-ion batteries dropped by 60%. China started facing overcapacity of lithium-ion batteries, and a race for the survival of the fittest began.

Karan soon had to find some way to survive in the market. He gave a new idea to the management to start contract manufacturing in China itself. Manufacturing in America or any part of the world except China could be more costly than in China. It was better to opt for contract manufacturing in China only. The idea was loved by his management, and they agreed. Karan's company had developed its unique chemistry and design, and it was better than the conventional chemistry. The prices of lithium-ion batteries had reduced so much that people looked forward to finding sustainable solutions from then on. And Karan himself could be seen on numerous conference floors, narrating his journey towards scripting the future in the world of energy.

He went further than just business in his commitment to clean energy. Karan took up the banner for the practice of sustainable lifestyles, advocacy for environmental projects, and working hand in hand with non-profits to educate people on renewable energies. He believed that change starts at the grassroots, and everyone has a part to play in making the future better.

Having left the company based in Abu Dhabi, he immersed himself fully in the subtleties of clean energy with the determination to carve out a niche in this relatively large field. His journey started with a deep dive into the renewable energy landscape—from solar and wind power to battery technology.

But still, Karan has to prove himself in the renewable and battery space. The market for green energy is big, but it requires a lot of support from large companies and the government. The transition we are talking about involves moving from one source of energy to another, and all the big companies, industries, and people have become accustomed to using fossil fuels. This Black Gold industry is at a very advanced stage compared to renewable energy, which is dependent on nature and is not as effective as Black Gold.

Karan was watching the market very closely, and he observed that sometimes the electric vehicle market went up in India and sometimes went down, but one market that was continuously growing was the Battery Energy Storage System market. Interest from private companies and the government could be seen in this sector.

The Indian government was floating many tenders, and more and more companies were participating each time in the Hybrid Solar & Battery Storage tender. Even more interest could be seen from bidders in the standalone battery energy storage system. Demand for lithium-ion batteries surged, though its growth was largely confined to a single sector. In another sector, which is bigger than automotive, demand was fluctuating, which would take time to stabilize.

Probably the most important learning that Karan picked up was the technology evolution. Because of innovation and shared knowledge, he could make things affordable for everyone in real life. Karan began forging connections with leading experts, researchers, and entrepreneurs at the forefront of clean energy. These contacts opened the door to new ideas and potential partnerships for the new venture.

Karan had a big vision. He did not just want to make batteries; he wanted to build an innovation center from which the clean energy movement could be further galvanized. For this, he needed a detailed plan, ranging from raising the funds and procuring raw materials to production line laying and quality checking. His efforts were ongoing in this direction. Karan was a person who understood oil and lithium. Karan was the person who understood black and white gold equally well. Karan's efforts were continuous in the direction of setting up the first gigafactory in India. His first step was to raise the funds. He had prepared the full plan, and his experience in the oil and gas sector would allow him to form a network of potential investors; it's only a matter of convincing them to invest in clean energy. He had prepared a full business plan with all the details concerning market potential, technological progress, and the environmental impact of lithium-ion batteries. His pitch wasn't just about profit; it was a call to invest in a sustainable future.

The work awaits for a greener and cleaner world, and Karan's efforts from the beginning will not go in vain. He had always proved himself in the worst conditions of war and sanctions. His ability to crack deals made him different from others. In clean energy, he had taken many initiatives, not only by himself but also by encouraging others to get into this sector. The world had also witnessed many climate change events in the last decade and faced a pandemic of coronavirus.

Everyone somewhere in the corner of their mind has understood that it's time to change from fossil to green energy if we want to survive for years and years. Karan's initiative in Green Ports and setting up a gigafactory will always be appreciated in the near future. Karan's plan was not only to set up the gigafactory; he wanted to bring the complete ecosystem of lithium-ion cell manufacturing to India. For this, he worked with many local companies to qualify them for cell manufacturing components like electrolyte , anode , and cathode.

He encouraged them, supported them with knowledge, and shared the gravity of this project.

Probably the greatest contribution of Karan was to developing countries. He realized that clean energy could change people's lives, especially those from parts of the world where access to electricity was not reliable. He worked with philanthropic organizations and government agencies to equip remote villages with solar power and battery storage systems to provide both clean and reliable energy to these communities, which until that point had been relying on dirty and unreliable sources of energy. He did not keep the clean energy agenda limited to India; wherever he had contacts or had worked before, he brought the clean energy revolution there with solar and battery solutions. This all started in a remote area of Africa, in Gabon, where he worked, and then in Lebanon, Jordan , and Iraq. These people had suffered from war, and Karan knew the feeling very well. He knew the true meaning of war and suffering.

Karan thought of integrating his batteries with solar and wind, creating fully customized energy solutions that could be proliferated for home, commercial, and industrial use. That approach was what made his company the differentiator in the sector, propelling it to the top in clean energy.

In each detail of the way he carried out his operations, Karan showed that he was truly committed to making a difference. To him, business success and social responsibility went hand in hand, and he worked towards building such a company. This approach didn't only guarantee his success but also earned him respect and admiration from peers. Endless opportunities appeared to Karan in the future. Clean energy was at its nascent stage, with ample opportunities for innovation and making a difference. He was especially eager to explore new technologies that would be the harbinger of change in the industry, including hydrogen fuel cells and advanced energy storage solutions.

Soon, Karan became synonymous with top-quality batteries. This success attracted new opportunities. Never in dispute with his principles of sustainability and ethics, and with an expanding business, Karan invested in R&D for constantly enhancing the efficiency and longevity of his batteries. Thus, he continuously ensured innovation, which brought a lot of changes in technology to his company and at the same time, success in the long term. Karan's path was, by no means, easy. The renewable energy business landscape was cluttered, with a need to remain on one's toes to stay ahead at all times. Regulatory changes, market fluxes, and technological breakthroughs – all had the potential to impact the business. Strategic thinking and a proactive strategy helped Karan pilot through these changes and challenges.

One of the major challenges was the changing regulatory environment: governments around the world were trying out policies on clean energy one after the other, but again, the policies varied and also changed quite fast. Karan had to keep attuned to these changes and make rapid adjustments to strategies, and more often than not, this posed an opportunity for lobbying for favorable policies and working with industry groups to influence legislation.

Karan's work in clean energy was much broader. Exemplifying this story was how he inspired many others to enter renewable energy and established his company as a model of sustainable business operations. He was asked to speak at conferences and events where he shared his story and insights. He stayed true to his commitment to clean energy through his other initiatives on the environment and his collaboration with nonprofits on clean energy education.

Chapter 10:
Landscape of White Gold

Karan's life was growing with the growth of white gold in India. New policies were being prepared to encourage investment in the white gold and renewable energy sectors. India was ready to see a new, clean, and bright future. Similarly, this trend was being followed around the world. India was looking for a big change this time, from an oil-dependent country to an oil-free country.

India imports 4 million barrels of oil every day, which creates an import bill of roughly 90 billion USD every year. Using a substantial amount of renewable energy with batteries could help cut a large amount of this import bill. And in no time, India understood the urgency of the situation. Suppose there is anything India has not enjoyed since Independence. In that case, it is the manufacturing of lithium-ion cells, and the country is putting all its effort into securing investment in this sector.

India has made huge progress in the last decade and under the new regime. Many new transitions like Digital India and AtmaNirbhar Bharat, creating a business ecosystem for investment, and the implementation of GST, which brought clarity to the tax system that used to be very complex in the early days, have made a new India and enabled it to make its position stronger on the world stage. Over the last decade, one document policy like the Aadhar card has made life easier for millions of Indians. Less paperwork and digitalization have been implemented at the ground level.

India, which has a population of 1.5 billion people with the largest diversity in culture, is both beautiful and complex. Lithium could help India in fulfilling several objectives:

Energy Independence: By having White Gold infrastructure, India could become oil-independent, catering to all its needs with solar and wind energy combined with batteries.

Green Commitments: This would make it possible to fulfill India's commitment to achieving 30% electric vehicles by 2030. This adds significantly to India's credibility as a future green country.

Export Earnings: Lithium is the most sought-after mineral in the world, and India can gain an export advantage by entering the global supply chain. Recently, India announced the discovery of 6 million tonnes of lithium in Jammu & Kashmir.

India has also found economic reserves of lithium in Rajasthan and Bangalore.

Employment: This discovery has the potential to create new employment and, in fact, transform the nature and role of the workforce in the near future.

Geostrategic Advantage: The most important advantage that policymakers could derive is avoiding dependency on China. Currently, India imports this crucial metal from China and Hong Kong. With its own reserves now, India can have domestic production and export earnings.

India must capitalize fully on this discovery. There shouldn't be gaps in planning or exploration. A well-guided mining strategy with reliance on sustainable mining practices and, most importantly, local involvement is much needed in regions like J&K. The green future, in the form of lithium reserves, has knocked on the door of India, and it is our duty to seize the opportunity and achieve the desired results.

As of today, modern civilisation is mainly coal- and petroleum-driven and has thus suffered much irreversible environmental damage. The solution that humanity sees lies in lithium-driven batteries, which could drive the next generation of our civilisation. Lithium is considered the tool for green economic transformation as its uses are diverse in renewable energy, such as solar panels, wind turbines, and electric batteries, all of which have started to change our environmental footprints.

Lithium batteries are long-lasting with high energy density, are rechargeable, and leave fewer carbon footprints. The metal also holds importance as it forms an important element in various industries as well.

According to a World Bank report, demand for lithium would rise by 500% by 2050. India has a vast land, the 7th largest in the world, which provides leverage to get the maximum sunlight to power our solar panels. India has a coastline of 7000 km where high winds blow, and installing wind turbines could help produce ample amounts of electricity. All this requires investment and infrastructure and cannot happen overnight. For companies around the world, India is a frontrunner in achieving its objectives in renewable energy. Every year, hundreds of megawatts of solar and wind power are added to India's installed power capacity.

The Indian government recognises the strategic importance of developing the 'white gold' industry, not just for commercial gains but also for military applications. To promote electric vehicles, the government is offering subsidies to electric vehicle manufacturers, which these manufacturers are directly passing on to the customers to benefit from.

The government is installing charging stations so that electric vehicle owners do not face any problems in charging their electric vehicles. There are sufficient charging stations in many metro stations, mostly located at petrol pumps.

The government has also incentivised the manufacturing of lithium-ion cells through the launch of its production-linked incentive policies in lithium-ion cell manufacturing. The government's offering includes 2.1 billion United States dollars in subsidies for 50 GWh capacity of lithium-ion cell manufacturing. The Indian government knows the value of developing the white gold business in India; it is not limited to commercial use but also has applications in the military.

These days, warfare relies more on technology than on human capability. Most wars are fought using unmanned drones and robotic equipment, and to power all of this, you need a high-power backup, which is only possible through lithium-ion batteries. Additionally, as there is often no grid electricity in very remote areas, these long-run lithium-ion batteries could play an important role.

Beyond the needs of every country, the bigger picture of using lithium-ion batteries is about climate. Climatic changes are taking place very fast, and there is a need to reduce our carbon footprint. Global warming is taking over everywhere; the temperature in colder regions is rising, and extreme drought and extreme rainfall are symptoms of climate change. The most important goal is to secure the ozone layer, which stops the UV rays from the sun. The ozone layer is depleting year by year, and if we continue to emit carbon, soon we will have a world with no ozone layer. A world with no ozone layer means catastrophe.

The colder regions are facing unimaginably high temperatures. Glaciers are melting rapidly. Low-lying regions near glaciers are getting flooded. The continuation of high carbon emissions is leading us to the destruction of human beings. There is an urgent need to save the climate, and all the countries are holding lots of conferences and seminars, both nationally and internationally, but the ground-level implementation is not even one-third of what we discuss in the big conferences. These days, almost all the major events like G7 or G20 have climate change as one of the top three key points of discussion. Developed countries have to commit themselves to bringing change at the ground level, not just at the event or seminar level. Developed countries have taken some initiatives, as they have allocated a good amount of funds and encouraged solar and wind companies to power the world with new sources of natural solar and wind energy. However, more than that, support is required; the transition requires strict discipline, and the carbon emissions of major companies need to be controlled.

Many companies have started reducing their carbon footprints through the process of producing their products. E-commerce companies like Amazon and Flipkart are using electric vehicles for last-mile delivery. They are using a fleet of electric vehicles for the delivery of their products, and telecom companies have started using lithium-ion batteries to power their networks instead of diesel generators.

Product-making companies are using biodegradable items and reducing plastic use, which are very welcome changes that we should further encourage. But are they sufficient to shake the world of black gold? Still, all the major power sources in India are from thermal plants that use billions of tons of coal, and in rural areas, many villages still use coal as fuel to cook their food. In the last decade, things have changed a lot. The government has reduced coal consumption and provided subsidies for LPG cylinders to rural areas. India contributes less than 4% of global pollution, while a major portion comes from the USA, which operates a large number of commercial aircraft carriers, aircraft, and other military equipment. Like the USA, there are several countries that burn millions of barrels of crude oil in their military defence operations. These are major causes of pollution; they organise drills and sometimes support wars actively or through proxy war.

This can only be stopped once a proper solution is provided, and all the countries come together and agree on it. 80% of global trade is conducted by sea, and large container vessels and tankers use HFO and MGO in port. Both are crude oil products and although maritime organisations have stricter regulations for lower sulfur and low carbon fuel, we are improving their quality. However, quantity-wise, consumption is increasing due to the large population of the world.

Karan has all these thoughts running in his mind, and he knows the solution lies in the evolution of technology and making it economically feasible. White gold is an expensive item that is available in vast quantities in nature. We need to have the right technology to purify it and make its application cheaper in the production of batteries.

There is no doubt that the world is trying, and everyone realised, some before the COVID pandemic and many after, that this is the only time to save the planet. If we do not act today, then we may never have the chance.

Many NGOs are working in this direction, educating people on the benefits of using clean fuel and batteries. Governments are exploring other clean energy sources, like biofuel, ethanol, and hydrogen. The government is running several programs on solar and wind energy. Solar power is now being provided in Africa, where there was no electricity. Solar energy is not just about clean energy programs; it is equally important in developing nations where the grid is not possible.

As the demand for AI and robotics increases, so does the demand for power daily. We cannot cater to this demand with thermal or fossil fuel, as this would increase carbon footprints and further destroy nature. Therefore, the need for clean energy is urgent, and this could be sourced from nature through solar or wind energy. The problem of energy availability could be solved with white gold through lithium in batteries.

The same applies to the space and data centre industries. We want a very advanced technology-driven world, and this is only possible with enormous power, which is only possible if we have it from a clean source, which is possible around the clock only with lithium-ion batteries and lithium. That's the reason lithium is called white gold, because of its critical importance in nature.

Lithium is white in colour, and its demand is equivalent to or greater than gold; hence, we call lithium white gold. If the human race wants to prosper, if the human race wants to survive in good health, and if the human race wants peace, then white is the colour for them—which is lithium—and green is the colour for them—which is solar and wind. This transition from fossil fuels to green energy, from black gold to white gold, is not just important; it is the need of the hour to move forward into the future.

Without it, the advancement of the world will not be possible, and nature is not in any state to bear more abuse from us. The world must change to avert catastrophe. If we want to give future generations a clean and breathable environment, today is the time for change. Not just one industry but every industry has to contribute to this change. Industries will have to figure out the process by which changes could lead to fewer carbon footprints. Recently, some steps taken by Europe for electric vehicles and green steel have been highly appreciated. All public transport should be converted from IC engines to electric vehicles. The world is ready to witness the biggest change of the century: transitioning energy sources from black gold to white gold.

It must happen for the existence of mankind, either by choice or by force.

Chapter 11:
Black Gold Vs White Gold

Karan believed that replacing black gold (crude oil) with white gold (lithium) required unyielding resolve and determination. This whole transition is not going to be easy. Despite the growth of white gold, the demand for crude oil has not decreased; in fact, it has increased.

The reason behind the increase in demand for crude oil is the two ongoing wars between Ukraine and Russia and Israel & Gaza. These wars fueled the increase in demand for crude oil as, generally, all the military equipment—tanks, aircraft, and armoured vehicles—are powered by crude oil, and nobody wants to take any chances with their security. All the military equipment runs on crude, and changing this requires a very big investment and the right technology in place.

While the world is eager to act, the real challenge lies in the supply response. For a long time, few strategists worried much about lithium supplies or the supply of lithium upgraded from its raw form to useful materials – an activity highly concentrated in China. Now they are. But what's interesting about lithium is how investors are responding. In 2022 alone, there was a one-fifth expansion in global lithium supplies – essentially all outside China.

In other critical materials, there are also big expansions of supplies away from today's dominant market suppliers—such as big new cobalt finds (instead of dependence on slave labour in Congo) and rare earth (in the US, instead of China).

In addition, new technologies for producing lithium have stronger incentives for proving today—such as extracting lithium from brines—which could be an important US supply. In all these areas, policies are helping encourage otherwise marginal supplies, but the raw market signal is also powerful.

When a new dependence on a material rises suddenly, there are all kinds of shocks and hiccups that translate into prices. Lithium prices and many other commodities soared amid COVID pandemic supply shocks, but they have since moderated. Lithium users, suitably shocked, are also finding other ways to lock up supplies, such as with longer-term contracts whose prices aren't directly reflected on spot markets.

The lithium market is very niche and in its early stages of growth. Various factors must be resolved as soon as possible to compete with crude oil. The most important thing is adaptability, which will come when you have infrastructure. You can't remove the IC engine from someone and replace it with an electric vehicle without a charging station. Nobody will accept this. We must avoid making this transition a burden on people; we cannot compel them to purchase costly electric vehicles

We cannot ask them to pay a higher price for their electricity bill simply because it comes from solar and batteries. The solution to each problem is the evolution of technology, which will reduce the cost of products, and the world needs to ensure a robust supply chain.

On the other hand, the oil and gas market is very mature. Two world wars were fought on the power of black gold. Initially, the oil industry faced hiccups, too, while extracting crude oil and refining it. Still, with the evolution of technology, it moved forward from onshore to offshore, from shallow wells to deeper wells, and from poor refining quality to high-grade crude oil. With higher technology, we controlled the carbon content in the ash, and we controlled the sulfur content in crude. Now, we have a world where wells can be drilled at 5000 meters in depth, and refineries can produce up to 10 PPM lower sulfur content. All of this happened through the evolution of technology, and the same is needed in white gold.

Technological evolution will reduce prices and open more opportunities for lithium mines.

The supply of lithium and control of its price is very important, and it should not be politically or geopolitically driven. Every country needs to ensure that this transition is not just for one country but for one planet, Earth. Every day, 100 million barrels of oil are produced globally to cater to the demand. We can understand how much carbon we emit by burning 100 million barrels of oil. Replacing such a massive amount of energy would be very difficult, but it is not impossible; it could be a dream come true for Karan.

This transition is like moving from land to sky. It has to be evaluated on many parameters: technology evolution, robust supply chain, adaptability of people, awareness, political and geopolitical considerations, and national and international perspectives.

It also needs to be advised and driven by people like Karan, who have worked in both the eras of Black Gold and White Gold. They understand better how this transition could take place swiftly and in the best possible ways. They understand the demand for Black Gold, the extraction of Black Gold, the refining of Black Gold, and the selling points of the same, and if it were replaced, how we could start filling those gaps with Green Energy and White Gold.

We need a person who is standing at the transition point of Black Gold and White Gold and who can see the future of both. Black Gold was the demand of the past, but White Gold is the demand of today and the future.

Support from world leaders is also required. More than support, we need commitment from them. Every year, a target should be set for the reduction of carbon footprints by every country, and it should be strictly implemented by the respective governments of those countries.

But what we see happening is the opposite. Oil production is increasing day by day, and oil companies' profits have doubled from last year, and this is because we are promoting war.

On one hand, we are talking about the Green Energy transition, and on the other hand, we are busy with war. How can these run parallel? No country is ready to compromise on the same. The number of wars, weapon production, and drills have all increased from the past. Industrialization is occurring, but not in a green way; it is still compatible with oil and gas. Countries are busy filling their strategic reserves, and yet we are talking about a green transition.

World leaders make grand speeches at events, but once they are back home, they talk of wars, which in turn increase the production of oil and gas. We need to come out of the mentality of War and Black Gold. War is not the future; it is destroying our future. The greed of a few will destroy the happiness of many. Our generation will pay the price for what we are doing now. With War and Fossil Fuels, we are creating a black world with no light and no hope, and the coming generation will never forgive us for the same. We will be responsible for creating their dark future; we will be responsible for their unhealthy future. What we received from our last generation was a greener world where we could breathe, a better world where we could celebrate, and a world where we could enjoy life independently. What are we going to give to our generations?

We need to make decisions soon. Time is ticking like a bomb. The effects of climate change can be seen everywhere: temperatures are rising, the ocean's water level is rising, and drought on land is increasing. The catastrophe is not going to see religion, race, colour, or wealth; it will be like the COVID pandemic. The same impact on everyone, and no wealth, religion, or race will save us from it. Lastly, Karan heard that the temperature at the core of the Earth has risen, and the spinning of the Earth is slowing down. Forests are burdened by excessive heat, as seen in Hawaii. These are warning signs, and it is up to us how we take them. We can improve ourselves to live longer or destroy the Earth.

Karan's initiative of setting up the first gigafactory to produce lithium-ion cells, setting up the complete ecosystem for cell manufacturing, and preparing the feed for cathode, anode, and electrolyte is appreciable. His latest initiative of setting up green ports and converting old ports into green ports has also been well-received by several governments in India and the Middle East, and both regions are working to implement it on the ground. Karan is in touch with large shipping lines to provide electric vessels and operators to provide green energy at ports.

People are following these initiatives, and demand for Electric Vehicles has increased in the last three years in both the Mobility and Storage markets. Battery manufacturers also have to ensure the safety of batteries, as in the past, many incidents of electric vehicles catching fire have occurred, which has slowed down the pace of this fast-moving sector. The safety of people is very important; nobody wants to risk their lives or the lives of their families during this transition. The transition is important but not at the expense of people's safety.

Strict policies need to be implemented by the government for using lithium-ion batteries so that people can have more confidence in them and increase adaptability. Infrastructure and safety are two crucial points for the adaptability of people to green solutions. Karan is sure that after the COVID pandemic, people have understood the value of life and the power of nature. It is invaluable, and we need to respect both. We need to teach our coming generation what we faced and how to act and face the change.

Karan knows that the challenge is big, and the White Gold sector is competing against the Black Gold sector, which has strong roots everywhere. All industries have become compatible with Oil and Gas, and all modes of transportation have become compatible with Oil and Gas, but disruption is needed as soon as possible to save us from calamity.

Despite all these challenges, Karan continues working to find a solution in the hope of seeing a brighter and greener future. His journey started with Black Gold, he lived through wars because of Black Gold, and he experienced some emotional incidents that made him think about White Gold. His journey was never easy, and he gained valuable experience working on land, sea, during war, and in peace. Now it is time to use that experience for a better and greener world. Karan has always been busy in his professional life, and many memories have made him think a lot about his future. Karan's personal life was also a struggle and was not an easy path. Somewhere along the way, you have to make sacrifices. Life is not easy for anyone. It gives a lot and it takes a lot from you. Karan is still chasing his dream of setting up gigafactories in India and the Middle East. He has completely transformed, and his objective is to see what best he can give to this world, what best he can do for his people, for his society, for this world, and for this planet. Karan is sure about this successful transition from Black Gold to White Gold as he navigates his journey towards a green and brighter world.

We need to act fast to make this transition from Black Gold to White Gold successful.

"First two world war were fought between the Humans on Oil and Gas but third world war would be fought between Robots on Batteries and AI"

www.ingramcontent.com/pod-product-compliance
Lightning Source LLC
LaVergne TN
LVHW041909070526
838199LV00051BA/2559